The Ark Angel

God bless!

By Matt Stewart

JAMS Publishing

Cover designed by Getcovers

Printed in the United States of America

First Printing, 2025

ISBN: 9798314446010

www.MattStewartBooks.com

For my brother, Andy, and my sisters, Natalie and Jackie.

May you turn to God when life gets hard.

Other books by Matt Stewart:

The Walk-On

The Man from KNEW News

Tripp in Time

Unique Eats and Eateries of Kansas City

The Kansas City Royals: An Illustrated Timeline

CHAPTER 1

I'll never forget the day I almost died. Or the stranger who saved me.

I can still taste the dirty lake water rushing into my lungs. I tried to breathe before my head came out of the water. Big mistake. Water replaced air and I panicked.

But first, let me set the scene. I am eleven years old. Adventurous. Bold. And bored.

My parents once again took me with them to spend the weekend at our lake house in the Ozarks, in southern Missouri. First, there's the three-hour drive to get there. Boring! Then there's the fact I have no one to play with. No one my age lives nearby. My mom is once again sitting on a deck chair on the back porch, reading a romance novel and working on her tan, while my dad builds something in his workshop. Dad spends all his time fixing the house. Hammer pounding. Saw and drill squealing. His tools make all kinds of weird noises as he patches this and re-planks that.

They ignore me. They tell me to go outside and play, so I do.

On this particular summer morning, I am pretending to be an outlaw who just robbed a bank. I am running away from the sheriff. I have a straw cowboy hat on my head and a bandana over my mouth. I have a cap gun in my pocket. I shot off all the caps the first day my mom bought it for me, so it's unloaded. But in my imagination, there's a bullet in every chamber. I hide behind a massive oak tree. There are a lot of big oak trees in the woods by the lake house. I perk my ears. I hear gunfire in the distance. The sheriff is getting closer. I grab my imaginary bag of money a little tighter and run to the next tree.

I know these woods well. Just last weekend, I ran through here to escape a dragon, though I actually ran off to escape my parents. They were yelling at each other. Again. They yell at each other all the time. I used to cry about it, but now I don't. It's like white noise to me. And it's so predictable. Dad will do something wrong. Mom will yell at him. Dad will yell back. Mom will cry. Dad will apologize. They do this almost every day. I wonder if they even like each other. I wish they would get along, but they don't. My friend Jimmy's parents are divorced. He said it's great because they spoil him with toys and kid's meals from fast-food restaurants. He has two beds and two homes and two sets of clothing for each home. He says it's cool. I guess I should embrace it. Divorce is inevitable.

I sprint down a footpath and swerve left and right to avoid the gunshots. The sheriff is getting closer. I turn back and fire my cap gun.

"BAM!" I yell.

Shoot, I missed. I jump behind a tree and lean into the bark. I'm breathing heavily. I feel a cramp building in my side. I blame the Pop Tart. Mom made scrambled eggs and toast for breakfast and told me I couldn't eat anything else until lunch. When she wasn't looking, I stole a blueberry Pop Tart. I scarfed it down fast so she wouldn't catch me. Now, I feel blueberry rising up in my throat. It threatens to come back up. I gulp, close my eyes, and relax.

Oh no! The sheriff is getting closer! I ignore the nausea and peek around the corner. He's hiding behind a nearby tree, waiting for me to come out. I look ahead and see the lake. If I can get to the water, swim to the community dock nearby, and avoid his bullets, I can get away with the money and live to see another day.

I'm a good swimmer. My parents taught me how to swim at an early age because they didn't want to watch me every time I jumped in the lake. They only have one rule: I must always wear a life jacket whenever I get in the water. I don't have time for that nonsense right now. The sheriff is on my tail. He'll shoot me dead if I stop to put on a life jacket. Besides, my life jacket is back at the lake house, way off in the distance. I don't want to go all the way back to the house to grab it. Being a strong swimmer, I have no fear. Besides, my parents will never know I got in the water without it. They can't see me from the lake house. It's too far away from here. I'll just swim to the community dock, rest, swim back to shore, dry off, and go home for lunch. No problem. I can do this in my sleep.

I look out at the water. 'It's not even that deep here,' I think.

But I am wrong.

I put my gun back in my pocket, pull the bandana down from my mouth, and sprint into the lake. My heart races as I imagine bullets whizzing by me. Sweat drips down my brow. My feet hit the warm water, and I keep running until the water reaches my chest. I then go into a side stroke. I feel the gun fall out of my pocket.

"No!" I yell.

I reach for the gun and feel the edge of my fingertips graze the handle. I lunge at it but miss, and it sinks. I take a deep breath and dive under the water to get it. I can't see anything. The water is murky. I pull myself down toward the bottom of the lake, grasping at the water, hoping to grab my gun before it hits the muddy bottom. I never feel the bottom. The wat88er is so deep here. I suddenly realize I can't breathe. I start to swim back to the top. Thinking I've reached the surface; I gasp for air. Big mistake. I'm still underwater. Warm water pours down my throat and into my lungs. I cough. I sputter. I keep swimming upwards. My head finally breaks the surface. I try to force air into my waterlogged lungs, but all that comes out is a moan. I panic. I flail. I see the shore. It's too far away. I see the dock. It's also too far away. I'm going to die. I'm going to drown. I turn to the dock and flail my arms, trying to will my body toward it, but I can't move. I feel my body sinking. I watch the sky disappear as my head sinks into the murky water. All goes black.

I am now floating above the lake. Floating? What? This is weird. I can actually see my body floating on the lake. My head Is under the water. Is this it? Is this the end of me? Suddenly, I see a young, athletic man run into the water to save me. He reaches into the deep and lifts up my limp body. I realize my soul has left my body. I am looking down on the world. I am a spectator. I watch this young man gently lay me on the beach, and he begins to press my chest. I stop floating on air and feel a tug pushing my soul back into my body.

Next thing I know, I'm coughing. Warm water flows out of my mouth and nose. I turn my head to the side and vomit. Chunks of Pop Tart and eggs and toast all pour out onto the sandy beach. I feel a warm hand on my back turn me onto my side. The hand begins to pat me lightly as I convulse a few more times. More food and lake water exits my body. My lungs and stomach hurt. I close my eyes and cry out in pain.

"There, there," I hear a warm voice say.

I roll back and turn my head to see the source of the voice. Who's patting my back? Is it my dad? Did he see me drowning and race over to save me? To my disappointment, it isn't him. Instead, it's a stranger. Someone I've never met before. Does he live nearby? Did he see me drowning from his back window and run over to save me?

This stranger looks to be in his mid-20s. He is muscular and handsome with a square jaw, hypnotizing brown eyes, and silky long brown hair. Like me, he is soaking wet. His white T-shirt sticks to his broad chest while his blue jeans look like they are painted onto his thick, muscular legs. Drops of lake water drip from his long hair. He smiles at me. His teeth gleam white. His large blue eyes emanate empathy.

"What happened?" I croak.

"You were swimming when you suddenly went under. I could see you struggling in the water, so I jumped in and pulled you out."

"Where did you come from?"

"I was walking on the beach and saw you go under."

"Thank you," I whisper as I wipe a tear away with my sandy hand.

"What's your name?" the man asks.

"Christian. What's yours?"

"Michael. But you can call me Mike. Where do you live, Christian?"

"My... my parents own the lake house over there." I point to an area down the beach. "You can't see it from here but it's not far. Have we met before?"

Mike looks familiar to me, for some odd reason. I can't stop staring at his warm, blue eyes.

"I don't think so," he answers. "Why don't I take you to your parents."

"No!" I say louder than expected. "I mean, they don't need to know about this, do they?"

"Are you afraid you'll get in trouble?"

I nod. "I'm supposed to wear a life jacket in the lake. I don't want my mom and dad to yell at me again. Can we just keep this between us?"

Mike leans back and smiles. Then he stands up, extends his hand, and helps me to my feet. He wipes the sand off my back, grabs my arms, and turns me around so I am facing him. With a look of warmth and wisdom, he says, "I want you to know something, Christian. Today wasn't your time to die."

"Thank goodness," I respond.

I feel his grip on my arms tighten. "You are destined for great things in this world, so stay safe and know God is watching over you."

"God?" I ask.

Mike points to the sky "The Big Man Upstairs. The Creator. He made you and has big plans for you."

I am confused. "How do you know?"

"I just know," Mike answers. "Christian, do you believe in God?"

"I don't know. My family doesn't go to church. My mom says God isn't real."

"If she doesn't think God is real, why did she name you Christian?"

"She said she loved the name Chris, but too many people were naming their kids Christopher. So, she decided to go with a unique name. Christian."

"It's a great name. By the way, your mom is wrong about God. He is real." Mike says it with so much confidence and assurance, it's hard to doubt him. Mike then motions to the lake and woods. "God created all of this. And you. It's pretty amazing, when you think about it. How did God do all of this? It's not important for you to know how. Just know He made you and loves you very much. He loves you so much, He sent me here to save you from drowning."

"He did?"

"Yup."

"Cool," I say.

"Go on home, Christian, and remember to stay out of the lake unless you're wearing your life jacket. I don't want to have to save you again."

"Okay," I answer. "I'll wear my life jacket from now on. I promise."

I give a small wave, turn around, and start walking back to the lake house. As I do, I realize my cap gun is still on the bottom of the lake. Did Mike grab it when he saved me? Can he find it for me? I turn around to ask, but he's gone. It's just me, standing on the beach alone. I scan the woods but don't see anything. I shrug and head home.

CHAPTER 2

Ten years later, Mike saves my life a second time.

I am driving fast. Too fast. I don't care. My girlfriend of four years just broke up with me and I'm mad. Furious, if I'm honest. I can't stop the tears from falling. I gave her four years of my life. I bought her a ring. I planned to propose on her birthday. But two weeks before the big day, she told me she didn't love me anymore. She said it wasn't me. It was her. That's what people say when they don't want to hurt your feelings. But I'm not dumb. It had to be something I did. Or said. I begged her to take me back, but she refused. She said she'd already started dating some other guy. So, I jumped in my car and started driving.

I'm driving down a deserted highway outside of Lawrence, Kansas. I'm a senior at the University of Kansas. A journalism major. I want to write stories – not for newspapers but magazines. I want to tell in-depth stories that enlighten readers while transporting them to another time and place. I'm excited about the possibilities. A future filled with adventure. That's what I loved about Anna. She wanted to do the same thing.

I look down at the speedometer and see the needle going past 80. I wipe a tear from my eye so I can see the road better. I space out as I remember the first time I met her.

It happened four years ago. I was standing outside the Student Union when I heard a clicking noise. There she stood, next to a pillar, her camera aimed in my direction. Taken aback, I stopped and stared while she took a few more pictures of me. Then she lowered the camera and smiled. Her bright blue eyes stole my heart the second I saw her. I looked behind me and saw I was all alone. I pointed at my chest and mouthed, "Me?"

She laughed. God, I loved that giggle. So innocent and pure. She pointed at me and nodded. Then she put the camera back to her eye and started clicking. I don't know what got into me, but I dropped my backpack and started giving her all kinds of goofy poses. I flexed like a bodybuilder. I stood on one foot and lifted my arm in the air like a ballerina. I gave her a Heisman pose. She kept clicking away, laughing. Soon, I was laughing, too. I grabbed my bag and walked over to her.

"Look at that. First day of class and I already have a stalker."

She raised an eyebrow and gave me a smirk. "How do you know I'm stalking you?"

"You were taking my picture, weren't you?"

"No. I was actually aiming at the guy behind you, but you got in my shot."

I looked behind me to see what guy she was talking about, but there was no one there. I felt her warm hand touch my arm, sending shivers through my body.

"I'm kidding. I'm playing with my new Canon EOS-1. My parents gave it to me as a gift. I'm just testing it out."

"Sure. Likely story. I think you became enamored by my manliness and wanted to preserve it on film for all time. I get it. I'm hard to resist."

She laughed again and put out her hand. "Hi. I'm Anna."

"Hi Anna. I'm Christian. Where are you from?"

"Kansas City."

"Me too! I went to high school at Olathe Northwest."

"Park Hill South."

"So, you're a freshman, too?"

"I am. What's your major, Christian?"

The way she said my name caused my heart to skip a beat. I couldn't stop staring at her translucent blue eyes. She radiated beauty with her short brown hair, long eyelashes, small nose and plush lips. She stood a bit shorter than me, maybe five-foot-four, but she had an athletic build which told me she liked to work out and stay physically fit. She looked ready to go for a hike in the woods in her khaki shorts, brown boots, and unbuttoned flannel shirt, which covered a blue KU Jayhawk T-shirt.

"I'm in the school of journalism. I want to write for a magazine like National Geographic."

"You're kidding me," Anna said with her mouth open. "I'm a photojournalism major, and my dream job would be to travel the world and take pictures for National Geographic!"

"There are just so many undiscovered things in this world," I commented. "I mean, to be the first to see a new bird species or see how the aboriginal people live in today's world. All of that fascinates me."

"Wouldn't it be amazing if we both ended up working for National Geographic and went on assignments together?"

I stepped back in mock horror. "That's a little presumptuous of you, isn't it? We just met!"

Anna laughed. "I guess I *am* stalking you. Want to get some coffee and talk more about it?"

How could I say no?

We walked into the Student Union, ordered coffee, and ended up talking for the next two hours. It all came so easy. Anna came across as very bright and wise to the world. No matter what topic I brought up, she had an educated opinion about it and could carry on an intellectual conversation. We agreed on many topics, except for faith.

"How can you not believe in God?" Anna asked me.

"I need to see some evidence before I believe in God."

"The evidence is all around us! The birds, the grass, the trees, us. I mean, what more do you need? The odds are extremely rare that this world spontaneously came into existence with humans at the top of the food chain. In fact, some of the most respected scientists agree that the very existence of our world proves there is a God."

"I guess," I said. "It just seems that some religions are pushy. They threaten their congregations with going to hell if they don't believe everything they say about God."

"You're right," Anna said. "Some religions are like that."

"Do you believe in hell?" I ask.

"I don't know. Kind of. I think really bad people go to hell, but I also believe that God loves all of us, no matter what religion we follow. I think God even loves people like you, you know, people who don't believe in Him."

"Okay, you've convinced me. I believe in God now."

Anna laughed. "Wow, you're such a pushover."

"Okay, then I won't believe in God."

"No! I want you to believe. Wouldn't you rather believe and be wrong than not believe and be wrong?"

"Great point," I say.

"What does it cost to believe in God? Nothing. And it makes me feel good. I like believing that God is looking out for me and protecting me from all the evils in this world."

I nodded my head. “That makes sense. Okay, I’ll believe in God, then.”

Anna reached over and squeezed my hand. “Good.”

But I was just telling her what she wanted to hear. Even after being with Anna for four years and going to church with her on occasion, I still struggle to believe in a higher power. I consider myself to be an atheist.

“By the way, I’d love to go out with you sometime,” I said to her when our first conversation ended. “Maybe dinner?” I held my breathe, afraid she would say she already had a boyfriend.

“Sure! How about tonight?”

I laughed. “You don’t waste any time.”

“Neither do you. Let’s just say, when I find something I like, I go for it. As my dad always says, ‘Life is too short for regrets. Live each day to the fullest, and don’t be afraid to try new things.’ It’s my life philosophy.”

“You have a life philosophy?”

“Sure. Don’t you?”

“Uh, yeah.” I racked my brain trying to come up with something clever, but all I could come up with is, “Don’t count your chickens before they hatch.”

Anna laughed. “I think it’s eggs. Don’t count your eggs before they hatch.”

"Yeah, that's what I meant." I turned red with embarrassment.

"What does that mean anyways?" she asked.

"It means even though I wanted to ask you out the moment I met you, I didn't count on it."

"Why not?" she asked as her eyes fluttered.

"Because you're too beautiful to go out with a slug like me."

"Oh, please. You are not a slug. In fact, I would venture to say you're better-looking than all the other slugs at this college. In an Indiana Jones kind of way."

I laughed. "All I need is a whip and a fedora."

"Let's not get ahead of ourselves," Anna smiled as she stood up to leave. "I'm in Corbin Hall. Room 330. See you at seven."

Anna grabbed her camera and took one last picture of me as I sat stunned by her beauty and forwardness. She turned and walked away, her hips swaying as she sauntered out of the Student Union.

Now I speed down a deserted highway overwhelmed with feelings of loss. Tears flood my eyes. I remember all the great moments we shared together. The intimacy. The laughs. Snuggling with her in bed. Studying together in the library. Eating ice cream on Mass Street. Holding hands as we cheered the basketball team from the student section. I was convinced she was the one. My future wife. I was so sure, I bought her a diamond ring. I could only afford a small one, but I knew she didn't care about the size or clarity of the stone. For Anna, it was all about the thought behind the action.

How did I not see this coming?

I frantically think about what I did wrong. How did I push her away? What did I do? What caused her to look for someone else? So many unanswered questions. I knew we'd been drifting apart. We'd both been busy. Anna worked at a local bar as a waitress. She'd been working extra hours to save for a trip to Egypt so she could take pictures of the Nile and pyramids and tombs where ancient pharaohs once laid. I'd been spending more of my time with my fraternity brothers, drinking most nights, showing up at her apartment drunk, even spending several nights on her bathroom floor, throwing up into her toilet. I still curse my bad luck when I literally ran into the cop as I left the liquor store with an unpaid bottle of bourbon in my hand. It had to be his easiest arrest ever. My friend, Jermaine, bailed me out, but then I omitted my arrest from the narrative when Anna later asked about my night. I didn't see anything wrong with that. I didn't want her to worry. I'm 22-years-old. I tried to steal the liquor on a dare. It's not like I have a history of crime. A history of public drunkenness. I'm just a young man having fun with my friends. But then she found out. She accused me of lying to her. She said she didn't want to date a thief and a liar.

"I'm so stupid!" I shout in the car as my foot falls heavier on the gas pedal. "Idiot! You have the most amazing woman you've ever met, and you lose her? Over alcohol? Over stealing? Damn you, Christian!"

The two-lane road ahead of me is very dark. Black. The headlights of my 1985 Dodge Charger barely light up the concrete ahead. I am the only one out here. Alone with my thoughts. My regrets. My sadness. I want Anna back. I want to tell her I'm sorry and ask for a second chance. Why do I feel like I'll never get one?

I am no longer alone. I see the eyes first. Yellow. Staring at me. It's a buck. His antlers sit wide and sharp atop the crown of his head. It freezes in the middle of the road. My lane. I slam on the brakes and turn the wheel hard to avoid hitting this animal. I feel my car take flight as it soars off the road toward a ditch. I feel weightless. Then my breath leaves my body, the seat belt tightens, and my car flips over into a ditch.

Darkness envelopes me.

I struggle to open my eyes. I'm groggy. Everything is fuzzy. My head hurts. My car is beeping. I smell sulfur from the deployed air bag. I hear someone open my car door. The metal on metal causes a loud screech. I feel a hand reach around me and unlatch my seatbelt. Hands grip my coat tightly around the shoulder and drag my body out. My vision returns. I see an orange and yellow light cutting through the darkness. I tilt my neck up to see my car upside down. Flames flicker from the bottom of it. My body hurts. I relax and let my rescuer pull me away from my burning car.

My savior is now kneeling over me.

"Are you okay?" the man asks. For some reason, his face seems very familiar.

"Yeah," I mutter. "I guess. What happened?"

"You crashed. I ran over to help you out of the car. Are you hurt?"

I move my arms and legs. I can feel them. My back aches, as does my head, but everything seems to be in working order.

"I think I'm okay. Can you help me sit up?"

I offer my hand, and he raises me to a sitting position. Now I can see the crash scene. My Charger is demolished. The entire top is caved in. The fire continues to burn but isn't getting bigger. How did I survive?

"I'm Mike, by the way," the man says.

I look at him for the first time. He is young and athletic with wide, kind brown eyes, a clean-shaven face, and long brown hair. He seems so familiar. Have I met him before? I can't place him.

"I'm Christian," I say. "I think I'm ready to stand. Can you help me?"

Mike stands up, grabs my hand, and gives me a boost off the ground. I grunt as I feel pain all over. I put my hands on my knees and take a deep breath. Panic builds up inside me. My car is totaled. I am stuck in the country. How will I get back? Did I crash on purpose? Did I want to die? Why is everything so fuzzy?

Mike puts his hand on my back for comfort. "Hey, deep breath. I know your car is ruined, but at least you're alive, right?"

I keep my head down and wipe a tear, not wanting Mike to see me cry. I take a second to compose myself and answer him. "I honestly didn't mean for this to happen."

"Of course not," Mike said. "If it hadn't been for that buck, you'd still be driving down the highway."

I look up. "How did you know about the buck?"

Mike smiles. "I told you, I saw the whole thing."

"But I don't remember seeing any cars on the road when it happened."

"Oh, I wasn't driving. I was walking."

"Walking?"

"I like to get out for a stroll now and then, and I just happened to be here when you crashed."

I look around and realize there are ditches on either side of the road. There are no sidewalks. No paths. This is not a place where people go for walks. A sudden pain jolts my head. I yell and rub my forehead.

"Here. Sit back down." Mike grabs my arm and helps me back to the ground. "It looks like the paramedics finally got here."

"But... how'd they know?"

"I called them right after it happened," Mike says. "How's your head?"

"It really hurts," I say.

Mike looks me in the eye. "You know, Christian, it wasn't your time to die."

Where have I heard that before?

I feel his grip tighten. "You are destined for many great things. Stay safe and know God is watching over you." Mike stands, turns toward the ambulance, and waves. "Over here!"

I suddenly feel really dizzy. The entire world is spinning.

I pass out.

When I wake up, I'm lying in a stretcher in the back of an ambulance, being taken to the hospital. The paramedics are asking me questions, but I am too tired to answer. I close my eyes again. I eventually feel the ambulance stop. The paramedics take me out of the ambulance and roll me into the emergency room. Doctors examine me, then leave. Once I am alone, I reach into my pocket and pull out my cell phone. I call Anna.

"Hello?" she says.

I can't control my emotions. I start to cry.

"Christian? Are you okay?"

"No," I cry. "I crashed my car and almost died. I'm at the hospital."

"What? I'll be right there."

Thirty minutes later, Anna is by my bedside. She leans over me with tears of happiness flowing down her cheeks.

"You're alive," she whispers.

I feel a wave of emotion overcome me. "I thought you broke up with me?"

"I'm sorry. I made a mistake." Anna says. "I love you too much to give up on us now. You're worth fighting for. Our future together is worth fighting for. After I broke up with you, I drove around Lawrence trying to find you to apologize and ask that we try again."

"But you said you were seeing another guy?"

"I lied," Anna says. "To hurt you. I'm sorry."

I squeeze her hand. "I'm sorry I hurt you with my drinking and my lying. I won't drink ever again. I promise."

She starts to cry. "You could've died tonight."

"I know. I'm sorry. I was so mad at myself for hurting you. There was a buck on the road. I had to veer quickly to avoid hitting it. I flipped my car and some guy walking down the highway pulled me out. He saved my life. He said his name was Mike…" I suddenly remember.

Anna looks at me curiously. "What's wrong? Are you feeling okay? You look pale."

"I remember Mike," I say.

"Remember him? From where?"

"He saved my life when I was a kid."

"What? Seriously? How?"

"Remember how I told you I once tried to swim to the dock at my parent's cabin and started drowning when a strange man jumped in and saved me?"

"Yeah. Are you sure it's the same guy?" Anna asks.

"Positive."

"But it doesn't seem plausible…"

"I know. But I swear, it's the same guy."

Did Mike remember saving me at the lake? I'm older. I look a lot different than I did at eleven years old. Man, I really want to talk to him, but I don't know how to find him. I wish I would've remembered him sooner. What are the odds of Mike actually saving my life twice in two different places? Astronomical, I would think.

I shake my head in amazement. "Apparently, I have a guardian angel, and his name is Mike."

CHAPTER 3

Twenty years after the crash, I am drowning in grief. I am sitting in a chair on the dock of my parent's former lake house, which is now my lake house. Anna and I bought it from them years ago. We spent every summer here with our son, Henry, as he grew up. We came here a lot during his childhood and made memories with him here. With Henry. Our son, who is now gone. Forever. Warm tears run down my face as I remember all the great times we had together.

I see his smiling face. How did I not know he was battling depression? How did I not see the signs? Why did he take his own life at the precious age of 18? Why? He had his whole life in front of him. I don't understand it. I want him back. Alive. But there is nothing I can do. What's done is done.

Was it my fault? Did I lead him to suicide? I feel guilty. We got into a fight right before he took his own life. He wanted to skip college after high school to work as a manager at a fast-food restaurant. I told him no; he needed to go to college to get a degree so he could have better career prospects. He didn't want me telling him how to live his life. We yelled at each other and then he left. He packed a bag and left our house. I begged him to stay but he refused.

The police found him two days later, dead in his car. I can't help but feel like I drove him to it.

Anna certainly blames me. She says if I had just controlled my temper and let him live his own life, he would still be alive today. I feel like I've lost my son and my wife. She won't speak to me. She is so deep in her grief, as am I. That's why I drove to the lake house. I need space to think. But I can't help but hate myself. I feel as if all of this is my fault. I wonder if taking my own life might make things better for Anna. Then she won't have to deal with me, the man who caused her son to take his own life.

I massage the cold, black metal handgun resting in my hands. It's heavy. Heartless. I look down at the Glock 19 and wonder what it will feel like to put a bullet in my brain. Will it hurt? Will I die quickly? Will I go to heaven or hell? If suicide is a sin, I have to be prepared to visit Satan in the fiery depths of hell. But I'm not afraid. Fire and brimstone? Bring it on. Grief eats at my heart. It tears away at my insides. I don't want to live anymore. I'm done. I'll accept the truth of whatever comes next, which I believe will be darkness. I don't believe in life after death.

I look up at the dark water in front of me and listen to the waves gently lap over the sandy shore. How many memories have I made on this dock? I remember jumping into the water countless times with Henry, laughing and singing and playing games. Since our travels with National Geographic took us away from him for weeks at a time during his childhood, we would make it up to him with trips to the lake.

I pop out the magazine in the gun to make sure it's loaded. It is. I click it back in and turn off the safety. I reflect on my life. I think about the trip Anna and I took to Cairo, Egypt, fifteen years ago. National Geographic sent us there to write a story on a newly found tomb in the Valley of the Kings. No one had stepped foot inside it since the pharaoh died. Anna took a ton of pictures while I interviewed Adom el-Sisi, the Egyptian archeologist leading the expedition. We'd worked with Adom on several stories in the past. When he and his crew discovered this new tomb, I was his first call. He knew having National Geographic publish the story would legitimize his find and help solidify his standing as one of the foremost experts on Egyptian history.

"I must warn you, Mr. Christian," Adom said. "There could be mountains of treasure inside or nothing but dust. We never know until we go inside."

"Even if thieves have already plundered this tomb," I say, "we'll still do an article on it. It's a remarkable story either way."

"I think so, too," Adom said. "But yes, I personally hope there is still treasure inside." I had always been impressed with how Adom left his home country to go to America to get a degree in archeology at Stanford, one of the best in the country.

Adom turned to the four men standing by the tomb's entrance and nodded. They grabbed their tools and began to chip away at the stone door frame. Another group of men stood nearby, knowing that when it started to loosen, they would be needed to help bring it down. The door to the tomb weighed hundreds of pounds.

Anna began taking pictures of the men working. Click, click, click. She moved away from me to capture them from a different angle. I'd always been so proud of her. I appreciated her talent behind the lens. She took immense pride in being creative, always framing her shots in unique ways while utilizing natural light.

As the workers continued to pound away at the door, streams of sand fell to the ground. Sweat poured down their faces and soaked their shirts as they intensified their efforts to loosen the stone door that had been sealed for more than 3500 years.

'I have the best job,' I thought as I watched in amazement. We would soon be entering a tomb that Adom believed was sealed back in 1480 B.C. After fifteen minutes of pounding on chisels, one of the workers said something in Arabic. The groups of workers waiting behind us handed the four laborers long metal bars. They placed the sharp ends of the bar in the crevice and hammered on the top of it. Soon, the bars slid through the crevice, creating a wider gap and loosening the stone door even more. The group of workers behind us then came forward and together, they pushed on the stone door until it fell forward into the tomb. A cloud of dust billowed into the entrance. I covered my mouth with a handkerchief until the dust settled. Then I peered into the darkness.

"Shuela!" Adom yelled.

Within seconds, a worker from the back of the group handed him a torch.

"La taqtarib!" He pointed to me and Anna. "I told them to stay back, but you two can come with me."

One of Adom's workers handed him a lit torch, and he went in first to light the way. I let Anna go in next. Her pictures were the most important part of the story. I followed her through the entrance and stepped on top of the stone door. We had to duck our heads to avoid hitting the stone ceiling.

"Ancient Egyptians were short," I said.

"Apparently," Anna said as she bent her 5'4" frame through the entrance.

Once in the tomb, we stopped to look around. Through the torchlight, I saw a room full of pots and dried food, clothing and furniture, all arranged neatly in rows.

"When the pharaoh becomes Ra and returns to the heavens, he must have all his possessions with him to fill his golden palace," Adom explained. "Come. The sarcophagus should be in the next room."

As I walked behind Anna through an open entryway into the next room, she gasped and quickly fired off a bunch of shots. I soon understood the reason for her reaction. Dozens of gleaming gold statuettes and jewelry surrounded a sarcophagus centered in the room. Next to it were four canopic jars with the heads of gods carved on the top. Inside were the pharaoh's internal organs: his stomach, liver, lungs and intestines.

"Help me," Adom said as he walked to one side of the sarcophagus. "Let us take this off."

It was a box in the shape of the pharaoh lying underneath it. I put my hands on either side, and we pushed. The lid barely budged. We added a little more muscle and slowly moved the lid to one side. We pushed on it until it tumbled to the ground. I looked inside the sarcophagus, stunned. Inside lay a gleaming golden coffin. I stepped back so Anna could take pictures of Adom next to his prize.

I smiled remembering the thrill Anna and I felt that night as we discovered a new pharaoh's tomb. Our article won awards and brought us name recognition. We started to get plumb assignments from the magazine. Rome. The Amazon. Pompeii. Moscow. We traveled all over. But poor Henry. Henry stayed home while we travelled the world. Fortunately, Anna's parents lived nearby. My parents were mostly absent, so Anna's parents watched Henry whenever we left on assignment. Maybe we shouldn't have left town so often. Maybe if we'd been home more, he wouldn't have...

The coroner didn't know if it was suicide or an accident. He didn't leave a note, so we would never know. All I knew is Henry opened my gun safe, took the Glock 19 I currently held in my hand, and fired it into his head.

"WHY!" I scream out into the night. "WHY DID YOU DO IT!!!"

Rage overcomes me. I fall into a trance and stare out into the black lake. I am out of tears. I realize if I'm going to take my life, I need to stop thinking about it and just do it. I have to simply raise the gun to my forehead without thinking and pull the trigger.

I point the gun toward me, tighten my grip around the handle, and slip my finger onto the trigger. I take a deep breath and start to raise my hand to my head when a voice interrupts my action.

"Christian!"

I jerk out of my trance and quickly lower the gun into my lap. I loosen my grip. The voice comes from behind me. I don't look. I stay quiet, hoping the person behind the voice can't see me. I hear footsteps on the wooden dock as the person walks toward me.

"I see you have a gun. Don't shoot. It's me, Mike."

Mike? I don't know any Mike.

"Go away," I mutter. "I want to be alone right now."

"I know you do, but I don't think you should be alone. I don't want you to do something you'll regret later."

"Please leave me alone," I say.

"I'm sorry, but I can't do that."

Now I'm mad. Angry. Who the hell is this guy and why won't he leave me alone. I figure I'll scare him away. I quickly stand up, turn around, and point the gun at the trespasser. The face I see shocks me. It's the same one I remember from twenty years ago pulling me out of my car. He hasn't aged a day. Tall and athletic, Mike wears a brown coat and jeans. He sports the same chiseled jaw and long hair I remember. His brown eyes emit the same empathy.

I drop my arm to my side as I process this moment. "Mike?"

"I'm glad you remember me. I wasn't sure you would."

"You saved my life. Twice. How could I ever forget you?"

"I saved your life three times."

"Three?"

"Right now. You were about to pull the trigger."

I look at the gun. No longer in the mood to end my life, I press on the safety and tuck it into the back of my jeans. "I don't understand. Why are you here?"

"To save you," Mike says nonchalantly.

"To save me? How did you know I was going to… did you follow me here?"

"Yes. I've been following you your whole life. I'm actually assigned to you."

"Assigned to me? What the hell are you talking about?"

"I'm your guardian angel."

CHAPTER 4

I stare at Mike, wondering what he means by "guardian angel". Is he claiming to be an actual angel or just a guy taking it upon himself to look after me? But if that's the case, why? I don't know him. He's not family. He's not even a friend. He's a stranger. None of what Mike says makes sense to me.

Mike's claim of being my guardian angel causes me to reflect on my faith. I'd like to believe in God, but I don't know. So many of my friends and family doubt the existence of God, and it's caused me to doubt, too. I don't know much about the Bible. I haven't spent a lot of time learning about Christianity. I barely went to church as a kid. When my parents did take me, which was typically only at Christmas and Easter, we went to a Lutheran church near our house. Honestly, I've always struggled with my faith. And yet this Mike-guy is claiming to be an angel? He looks human to me.

"I don't see any wings on your back," I remark sarcastically. "Or a halo over your head."

"That's because you're seeing me in my human form. If you saw me in my angel form, you'd see my wings and halo."

"Can I see you in your angel form?" I ask, wanting proof.

"Not now. Maybe later," Mike says as he looks around. "I wouldn't want anyone living nearby to see me in my angel form."

"But there's no one out here. Just us."

"Yes, but there are lots of homes nearby. And we angels emit a lot of light. I'm afraid someone would catch a glimpse of me, which would be bad."

"Why would that be bad?"

"Because God doesn't want us angels showing ourselves to humans."

"And yet, here you are, showing me your human form."

"This is different. You're different."

"What? How am I different?"

"You sure do ask a lot of questions."

"I'm a journalist. What do you expect?" I shake my head in disbelief. "Are you okay? I mean, mentally? You know, angels don't really exist, right?"

"Oh, but angels ARE real. You're looking at one."

I laugh and shake my head again as I try to make sense of what he's saying. "Whatever. So let me get this straight. After you saved me from drowning in this lake when I was a kid, you took it upon yourself to keep an eye on me?"

"I've been watching over you since the day you were born," Mike says.

"Why? Do you know my parents?"

Mike shakes his head.

"So, you've been stalking me my whole life?"

Mike laughs. "Not stalking. Watching over. God assigned me to you before you were born. My job is to watch over you and make sure you don't die before your time."

"Wait. Did you just say God assigned you to me? Come on!" I sat in silence, digesting all Mike said. None of it made sense. I truly don't believe in angels. I'd heard of angels but always assumed they were mythical creatures, like Bigfoot or the Loch Ness monster. Fun to imagine but not real. And yet here is Mike, mysteriously showing up in my life for the third time, saving my life, claiming to be an angel.

"So, you seriously want me to believe you're an angel?" I asked.

"Yes, I'm an angel from heaven." Mike smiles, showing patience with my confusion and doubt. "I know it's hard to believe. This world wants you to think it absurd to believe angels exist, but that's by design. God doesn't want us angels intruding in your life, so we stay hidden. It's my job is to protect you from the constant dangers you face."

"Constant dangers? Like what?"

"Some are obvious. Like when I saved you from drowning or pulled you out of your car after your car accident back in college. But many other dangers you've faced in your lifetime aren't as obvious. By my calculations, I've saved you from dying 987 times."

"987 times?"

"You don't realize it, but there are times I've hidden your car keys to delay you from leaving your house to prevent you from getting into a car accident. Just last week when you were walking on the street, I urged you to get on the sidewalk. And you did."

"You mean when that car came speeding around the corner and jumped the curb and nearly hit me?"

"Exactly, he would've hit and killed you if you hadn't been on the sidewalk."

"But how did you urge me to get on the sidewalk? You weren't there."

"Oh, but I was. You just couldn't see me," Mike explains. "You know how sometimes you get a gut feeling and your intuition tells you to do something? That's how we angels communicate with you. It's how we lead you in the right direction. When you listen to us through your instinct, good things happen. When you ignore it, bad things typically happen. I told your gut to get on the sidewalk, you did, and once again you avoided death when that driver jumped the curb."

"So, whenever my instinct tells me to do something, that's you?"

"It is."

"Hmmm." I don't quite believe all he's saying, but I must admit, he's a convincing storyteller. I wonder if this man is mentally unstable. How can I get him to leave?

"It's actually quite amazing how often a person should die during their lifetime," Mike says. "This cruel world is filled with evil and all kinds of threats, but you're none the wiser because I take care of you. For example, take your trip to Egypt 15 years ago with Anna. When you both uncovered the pharaoh's tomb. I know you were just thinking about it."

I gasp. "What? You can read my mind?"

"Of course. I always know what you're thinking. Anyways, remember when you crossed the Nile and floated into a herd of hippos? Remember how one of those hippos bumped into your small boat and you almost went overboard? Anna's guardian angel gave her a boost of strength and she grabbed your shirt to stop you from falling in."

"Wait, Anna also has a guardian angel?"

Mike nods. "Everyone has a guardian angel. We work together to protect people. As Anna's guardian angel gave her the strength to keep you from falling into the water, I stood in front of you to help you keep your balance. You couldn't see me, but I was there."

"I remember. That was one of the scariest moments of my life. I thought for sure I was going to die." How does he know all this? He wasn't there. I am now starting to believe that maybe he *is* an angel.

"You would've died had you fallen overboard."

"Okay, I'm obviously hallucinating right now. There's no way I'm talking to an angel from heaven. Please tell me I'm dreaming. That I'll wake up in bed and realize none of this is real."

"Oh, all of this is real," Mike says as he takes a step toward me. "Can we go inside? We have a lot to discuss."

He offers his hand and helps me up from the wooden dock. I am confused. I now want to hear what he has to say. Why not? What if he really is an angel? How amazing would that be!

From the dock, we walk on a trail trampled by many years of use. We go up a small hill, past leafless trees, inside my lake house. As I open the door and turn on the lights, a draft of warm air hits my face. It feels comforting to escape the fall chill. I take off my coat and hang it on a peg by the door. I walk to the couch in the next room, put my handgun on the side table, and sit down on the couch with a heavy sigh. Mike shuts the door behind him and sits in a soft recliner opposite me.

"This is nice," he says as he gets comfortable. "It's quite soft."

"I'm sorry, I'm being rude," I say as I stand up. "Would you like something to eat or drink?"

"Actually, yeah. I'm starving," Mike says as he, too, stands. "What kind of food do you have?"

"Wait. Do angels even eat?"

"No," Mike answers. "But I'm not an angel right now. I'm human. And all humans need food for energy." He follows me into the kitchen. "I haven't tasted food for many years. It's been a while since God allowed me to come to this world in human form."

"How long?"

"Before becoming human to save you? About two-thousand years."

"What?" I laugh. "Two-thousand years? Are you kidding me right now?"

"No, I don't kid. But keep in mind, two-thousand years in angel time is really not that long, since time doesn't exist in heaven like it does here on earth. Still, it's been a while since I've tasted food on this earth. When I saved you those two times, I didn't stop to eat."

Mike scours the counter and sees a box of Twinkies. He grabs one, unwraps the packaging, and takes a big bite. He then closes his eyes and smiles.

"Wow! This tastes really good!"

"You've never had a Twinkie before?" I ask.

"Twinkies didn't exist two-thousand years ago. What's this?" Mike sees a box of apple-flavored granola bars and unwraps one. He takes a bite and smiles again.

"This tastes great, too! Mmm, I miss being human!" Mike opens the refrigerator and takes out a Diet Coke. "Do you mind?"

"Of course not," I say.

Mike pulls the tab and takes a big gulp. He scrunches his face and emits a loud burp. "Sorry about that!"

I laugh. "I'm guessing you've never had carbonated soda?"

"Nope. But it's delicious!" Mike takes another gulp and looks back in the fridge. "What else do you have in here?"

"We only come to the lake house a few times a year, so I don't have anything perishable, since it would spoil." I reach into the refrigerator and grab a packaged peanut butter and jelly sandwich. I open it and hand it to Mike. "Here. Try this."

Mike takes a bite. "All this food tastes so good!" he says with his mouth full. "The last time I was human, when I was hungry, I had to dig up roots and search for berries, or kill an animal and cook it over a fire."

"We have factories now that do all that. Food has come a long way since then," I say.

Mike grabs the half-eaten Twinkie and granola bar, along with the sandwich and soda, and walks back to the chair in my living room. I follow and sit on the couch. Mike puts the food on a side table and continues to eat.

"Who knew eating could bring such pleasure!" Mike said.

"Maybe you should inhabit your human form more often."

"Maybe."

"Sometimes, I wish we didn't have to eat. So many people are battling obesity, eating food that's not good for their bodies. Sometimes it feels like our lives are always focused on our next meal."

"Ah, but think of all the flavors you'd miss out on if you didn't eat," Mike says. "Besides, hunger is one of the challenges God wants humans to experience."

"What do you mean by that?" I ask.

Mike stuffs the rest of the Twinkie in his mouth and says, "The whole purpose of life, the reason you exist in human form, is to face various challenges. God wants to see how you handle them. How you face these challenges forms your character."

I look at the gun on the side table. "I guess I lack character considering I just tried to kill myself."

Mike looks at me with empathy in his eyes. "You're not the first person to fail a challenge. What's important now is how you respond to this failure. Do you give up on life? Or do you learn from your mistakes and become a better person? The choice is yours."

I lean back. "I thought I wanted to die but now I'm not sure."

"Great! Then learn from it and do better." Mike turns and looks at a picture on the side table. It's Anna, Henry, and me smiling as we pose on the dock. "You have a beautiful family."

"Had," I correct him. "If you truly are my guardian angel, you would know that my son recently took his own life. Now my wife wants nothing to do with me."

"That's where you're mistaken," Mike says. "Anna still loves you and needs you now more than ever."

"But Anna told me she doesn't want me around anymore."

"People say hurtful things when they're grieving, but they don't necessarily mean them. Anna didn't mean it. I promise."

My heart feels a little lighter wanting to believe him.

Mike looks up from the photo. "I'm sorry about Henry."

I can't control my anger. "Are you? Really? Then why didn't you stop him? Why didn't his guardian angel stop him? Henry's guardian angel failed him!"

"Henry's guardian angel tried to convince him not to take his own life, but in the end, Henry made his own choice. I told you, we angels aren't allowed to make decisions for you. All we can do is lead you on the right path by tapping into your intuition and hoping you make the right decision. People make wrong decisions every day. Henry's not the first. If it brings you any comfort, you should know that Henry's soul lives on in heaven."

I am overwhelmed with a sense of hope. "Wait. Henry's in… in heaven?"

"Yes, he is."

"Even though he took his own life?"

"Yes. I've talked with him, and he's filled with regret. He's sad that he disappointed you and Anna and left this earth before his time. He's still processing those emotions in heaven, and someday you'll be reunited with him."

"Oh, my God," I cry, wanting to believe my only son is in heaven despite his actions. I feel my whole belief system changing at this moment. Anna always said it cost nothing to believe in God and heaven. I want to believe right now more than anything, so I decide I will. I will throw away all my years of disbelief and go all in on God.

Mike gives me a few seconds to regain control of my emotions before he continues. "Henry made a mistake in taking his own life, but that doesn't mean he should be punished for all eternity. God is love. He loves all His creation, even those who make mistakes."

"Like me?"

"Like you. I know all of this is confusing and scary and strange for you, meeting an angel."

"I don't get it," I say. "I've spent my whole life not believing in God, not believing in angels, and yet here you are. Why are you helping me when I never believed in you?"

"Because I've always believed in you," Mike says. "What you believe or don't believe doesn't change the truth. Now you know the truth, that God and angels truly do exist. It's okay to change your mind. Leave your doubts behind. I promise, God and I do not hold them against you."

I smile. "Thank you." I can't believe I just changed my entire belief system! But how can I not, given the evidence Mike is laying out in front of me. He knows everything about me. He's convincing. Plus, he did show up out of nowhere to save my life three times.

"I need you to trust me," Mike says. "Trust that I will protect you and guide you through the mission God has set for you."

"I'm sorry, what?" I ask. "God has a mission for me?"

Mike smiles. "He does. God chose you for this mission before you were born. When you were still a soul in heaven."

"He did? What do I have to do?"

"Not much. Just save the world from being destroyed."

CHAPTER 5

"I'm, sorry. What did you say?" I ask Mike.

"Your job is to save the world. I don't know if you've noticed, but this world and many of the people living in it have fallen into sin. Many don't believe in God, and many are hurting others for their own gain."

"But isn't that the entire history of humanity?" I ask. "We've always been cruel and hurtful toward each other."

"Yes, but it's worse now than ever. God is now seriously deciding whether to destroy this world and start over."

I sit up at the end of the couch. "Are you serious?"

Mike shrugs as if it's no big deal and drinks the rest of his Diet Coke.

"What do I have to do?"

"I don't know yet."

"You don't know yet?" My heart races with anxiety. God wants me to save the world? And my guardian angel has no idea what I have to do?

"God will tell me in due time and when I know, I'll let you know. Mind if I grab another Twinkie?"

"Go ahead," I say as I contemplate all he just said. As Mike walks back in the kitchen, I yell, "How can you be so nonchalant about all of this? God wants to destroy the world, and you have no idea what I have to do to save it? I thought angels knew everything."

"Not everything. God does keep some things close to the vest. But trust me. God is not crazy about the idea of destroying the world, but He needs things to change for the better – fast – or else He *will* start all over again." Mike walks back into my living room, eating a Twinkie. "I can tell you're worried. It's okay. Calm down. Even if God does destroy the world, your soul will still go to heaven. It's just the world He will destroy, not you."

I lean back and think of the consequences of our world being destroyed by God. "But think of all the history that would just disappear."

"Oh, it would be devastating," Mike says.

"And it's all on me to save this world?"

"That's what God tells me."

"And you honestly don't know what I need to do?" I ask.

"Nope," Mike mumbles with a mouth full of Twinkie.

As Mike sits back down in the recliner and licks his fingers, I contemplate my situation. It's so surreal talking to an angel. Since I have him one-on-one, I decide to ask him some other questions. Maybe I can later write an article on angels for National Geographic.

I look at the gun sitting on the side table. "I still don't understand something. If God let you stop me from taking my own life, why couldn't Henry's guardian angel stop him from taking his life?"

"I told you, angels aren't allowed..."

"I know, I know, angels can't interfere. But why not? Do you know how much tragedy would be avoided if angels interfered more often?"

"Christian, if we interfered and always saved our assigned souls from tragedy, you wouldn't have a life. You'd be a puppet. We would control you, always telling you what to do and where to go. Life would be boring, and you'd resent us for taking away your free will. Plus, your soul would never grow because you would never face adversity."

"But you've interfered in my life three times to stop me from dying," I say.

"Only because God needs you to stay alive. Again, you have been chosen by God, which means right now, you are the most important soul in the world. I'm not saying other souls don't have value, but right now they're not as valuable as you. Remember, every single soul has a guardian angel guiding them. God only allows us to nudge our souls in the right direction."

"Do you ever talk to God?" I ask.

"Yes, I do. God and I are very close. We go way back."

"What's God like?"

Mike smiles. “God is love, joy, and life all rolled into one. It’s the best way to explain Him.”

“Why did God create us in the first place?”

Mike smiles. “Man, you are relentless. Let me ask you a question. Why do you write magazine articles? Why does Anna take pictures? Why do people create music, paintings and sculptures? Because when you create something, you feel a sense of joy. It’s the same with God. He gets joy out of creating souls and deciding which bodies they should live in. God also derives great joy in watching His souls evolve and reach their potential through the living process.”

“But if God loves all His souls, why does He let bad things happen to good people?”

“God doesn’t *let* terrible things happen. Bad things simply happen because this world is filled with all kinds of obstacles. For instance, take Satan. He lives in this world. This is his domain, and his demons are constantly trying to lead people astray, tempting them to do dreadful things. Also, when God created this world, He set in motion certain natural laws that can cause natural disasters. Take earthquakes. God doesn’t cause them to happen. They happen because the tectonic plates are constantly shifting, a natural law He set in motion billions of years ago when He first made this world. Since God takes a hands-off approach and simply observes how souls navigate these challenges in this world, sometimes terrible things do happen to good people. But because God grants you free will, sometimes it's your fault, not God's. Sometimes your choices unintentionally hurt others. And sometimes people intentionally do terrible things to others.

"Your purpose in life is to feed your soul with knowledge and experience so you can make better choices. Make the wrong choice, and the energy surrounding your soul dims. Make the right choice, and it burns even brighter. Every decision you make in your lifetime contributes to the overall health of your soul. When this life ends, what's left? Your soul. Your essence. That's what goes to heaven. Not your body. Not your human shell. It's the soul inside your body that lives on."

Mike continues. "Yes, I'll admit God made life challenging. He doesn't come out and explain everything. He leaves it for you to figure out. That's why there are so many religions. So many opinions on so many topics. So much conflict. Humans have been trying to decipher God's intentions for centuries, and people will continue to make mistakes as long as this world is spinning. But we have finally come to a tipping point, Christian. We've come to a point where this world's future is in doubt, and God is struggling to see a path where this world can heal without intervention."

"And that's where I come in?"

"Exactly. Throughout the course of history, God has sent prophets to this world to help people see the light. To see the truth behind their existence. Their reason for being here. Prophets have course-corrected the fate of humanity for centuries. While God does take a hands-off approach to this world, when He sees things going in the wrong direction, He doesn't hesitate to interfere. Heck, He even sent His Son down here two thousand years ago to get the world back on track. And in some ways, it has. In other ways, it's gotten worse. Basically, God needs another prophet right now, and as luck would have it, He chose you."

CHAPTER 6

I laugh. I can't get over the absurdity of it all. Me? A prophet? Please! The claim is so unbelievable to the point of outrageousness.

Mike sits with a grin on his face. He takes a drink of his soda and smacks his lips. "As crazy as it sounds - and I know it sounds crazy to you - it's the truth. God chose you before you were born to take up this task. Of course, you still have a choice. You still have free will. You can say no, I'll disappear, and you'll never see me again. Or you can say yes and become a prophet and help God save this planet and everything on it."

"You know I don't go to church," I say.

"Going to church is not a prerequisite for this position."

"It feels like it should be. How can I share the Christian faith with others when I don't know a lot about it?"

"Being Christian is also not a prerequisite. Can I tell you an uncomfortable truth?" I lean in, interested in what Mike's about to say. "Every religion leads to the same God."

"Really?"

I think about his statement. How many religions threaten people with a ticket to hell if they don't believe in their faith to the letter. 'If you don't believe this, you'll get to hell,' they say. To think that Muslims, Hindus, Buddhists, Jews, and everyone else all pray to the same God is a concept I never really considered.

"It goes without saying, some religions are closer to the truth than others," Mike continues. "For instance, there is just one God. So, the fact some faiths believe in multiple gods is not true. However, when they pray to their gods, God hears them. Also, everyone, regardless of their faith, has a guardian angel. It's not like we're split into different religions. All guardian angels come from the same place. When humans die, their souls all go to the same place. What you believe during your time here is not as important as how you live your life."

"Whoa!" I say as I put up my hands. "What you just said flies in the face of conventional Christianity. Most Christians say if you don't believe in a Christian God, you'll go to hell."

Mike shifts in his chair. "You've touched on another one of God's frustrations. People are so quick to judge others and damn them because they're different or have a different point of view. It's an ugly side of humanity. God simply wants people to love their neighbor and leave the judging to Him. Just because your neighbor practices different faith from you doesn't mean he's going to hell. God created everyone in this world, and He loves all of His creation equally."

"Many religions would disagree with you."

"Yes, they would. But you must remember, what you believe doesn't change the truth. Take Santa Claus."

"Santa Claus?" I smile.

"When you were a kid, you believed Santa Claus was real. Your whole belief about Christmas centered around a fat man in a red suit climbing down your chimney to give you presents. When you learned Santa wasn't real, did any amount of belief on your end change the truth? No. It's not like the harder you believed in Santa, the more it became true. You simply had to adjust your way of thinking to understand that Santa was never real. It's the same with people and their faith. People want to think they know the truth about God, and they judge others using that 'truth' as a frame of reference. But the truth is, God is the God of all people. God created all people. God loves all people. If people would realize this, they could stop judging others and focus on their own soul's development."

"You sound a little upset," I say.

"I am. I'm tired of people acting like they know where a soul will go after death. Only God decides that. So many people act self-righteous, believing God will favor them because of what they believe and not because of how they live. It's egotistical and honestly, hypocritical to think you can sin all you want in life and believe God will automatically forgive you because you believe in Him."

"So, everyone goes to heaven? No matter what?"

"Let me put it this way. Everyone who WANTS to go to heaven after death can go to heaven. God doesn't damn souls to hell. If you go to hell, it's your choice, not God's."

"But why would anyone choose hell over heaven?"

"You'd be surprised," Mike says. "Some people are so filled with guilt and regret about their actions on earth, they don't feel like they deserve God's forgiveness. But hell is not what you think it is. There's no fire and brimstone. It's more of a type of purgatory. When a soul refuses to turn to God's light, they end up stuck in purgatory until they can learn to forgive themselves. This is why it's so important to live a good life, so you'll be ready to accept God's love and forgiveness when you die."

"You act like I'm at risk for being stuck in purgatory."

"I hate to say it, but you are. You harbor a lot of guilt. You almost took your own life tonight. If you had committed suicide, then yes, maybe you would've ended up stuck in purgatory. Not by God's choice but by your choice. You have so much anger in your heart."

I think about my son and once again feel as if I'm the reason he took his own life. Sadness, anger, and depression once again overwhelm me. I struggle to control my emotions.

"Christian, it's not your fault Henry committed suicide," Mike says softly.

"But I feel like it is," I cry. Tears rain down my cheeks. "I could've been a better father. I said some hurtful things. I should've seen he was depressed and stopped him."

Mike stands up, walks over, and puts his hand on my shoulder. "Henry made a choice, and there's nothing you could've done to stop him. It's not your fault. Honestly. You need to forgive yourself and not let his death eat at your soul."

"But it's so hard! I loved him so much. I miss him so much." I put my face in my hands and bawl.

"I know," Mike says.

Through closed eyes, I see a soft white light on my left side. I open my eyes and look at Mike's hand on my shoulder. It's glowing. A soft white light connects his hand to my shoulder. A sense of peace and calm fills my heart. I stop crying.

"What are you doing?" I ask.

Mike raises his hand and the light disappears. "Sorry, I was just calming your heart."

"Don't be sorry," I say, amazed by what just happened. "It worked. Thank you."

"You know, life is supposed to be hard," Mike says. "God wants it this way. If He didn't, He never would've created this world. Instead, He would've kept every soul in heaven."

"But why? Why put us through so much pain and suffering? What's the point?"

"As I said earlier, pain and suffering forces your soul to grow. You're only in this world for a short time, and the adversity you face causes your soul to evolve. Life is full of joy and pain, love and hate, good and evil, ying and yang. You can choose the good path and improve the lives of those around you or the selfish path and hurt others. Most people walk both paths throughout their life. But the more time you spend on the right path, the more you realize that goodness is all that matters. When you help others, love others, and care for others, you benefit in many ways. It helps strengthen your soul."

My head hurts. I close my eyes and rub my temple. "I am so overwhelmed right now," I say. "You're blowing my mind." I ball up my hands, put them at my temple, and open my fingers while making an explosion sound.

"I'm preparing your mind for the mission God has planned for you. We'll have more conversations in the days ahead, but right now, I have to go."

"Go? Where?" I ask.

"Back to heaven. I have to go back to being your guardian angel," Mike answers. "But before I leave, I need you to do something."

"What's that?"

"I need you to go home and make up with Anna."

My heart drops. I know she's still mad at me and blames me for Henry's death. "You sure she'll take me back?"

"She will, but it won't be easy. You'll have to open up to her and speak from your heart. By the way, before I leave, can you get me another soda?" Mike asks.

I stand up and walk into the kitchen, contemplating all I will say to Anna when I see her. How can I earn her forgiveness? I grab a soda from the fridge and head back to the living room.

"You know, Mike, I could certainly use your help buttering her…"

I look around but Mike is gone.

"Mike?"

Silence.

I walk to the window and look outside to see if I can catch him walking away. A part of me still struggles to believe he's an angel. I then imagine Mike floating near me, invisible, with wings on his back and a halo over his head, watching over me.

I sit down, open the soda, and take a big gulp. Did I really just have a conversation with an angel? I contemplate all God might want me to do as His prophet. What will I have to do for God? The possibilities excite and frighten me at the same time. But what choice do I have? Mike said God assigned me this task before I was even born. Wow. To think that God chose me, of all people. Me!

I go to the bookshelf and pull out the only copy of the Bible I own. I figure I should do some research. I sit back down on the couch and open it up to the first page. What a thick book! It's going to take me some time to read it all. I look down and start with the first sentence.

'In the beginning…'

I pause. My instinct tells me to call Anna. Is that Mike talking to me? He said it was how he'd communicate with me. I listen to him, pull my cell phone out of my pocket, and give her a call.

CHAPTER 7

I sit at a table with a steaming cup of coffee near my right hand. I am alone, waiting for Anna to arrive. Across from me sits a stemmed glass of her favorite cabernet. I hope wine might encourage her to forgive me.

I've picked a table near the back at Jasper's Italian Ristorante. I take a sip of coffee and reflect on my conversation with Anna the previous night. She stayed mostly silent while I begged her to meet me here for dinner and conversation. She reluctantly agreed, proving Mike right. But would she forgive me? I still had a lot of apologizing to do.

I contemplated our marriage. I analyzed it. I tried to figure out how we went from being inseparable to distant. Before Henry took his own life, Anna and I were tight. Our marriage was rock solid. But afterwards, in the days after his funeral, we let our anger and sadness get the best of us. We started shouting at each other. Pointing fingers. Blaming each other. I'm sure suicide has done that to many a couple. It's easy to blame the other person, though it isn't necessarily fair. I figure it's natural to want to vomit your anger on someone, and that someone is usually someone you love.

I look around the restaurant, wondering if Mike might show up for dinner. I don't see him. When will I see him again? I smile, imagining him showing up in human form just because he wants to taste the pasta. I can't believe it's been more than two thousand years since he's come to earth in human form. I imagine him standing behind me as I sit. Knowing Mike is with me boosts my confidence. He said Anna would forgive me, so all I can do is trust he is right.

I look toward the front door, but Anna doesn't walk through. She hasn't arrived yet. While I wait, I let my mind wander. I think about my trip earlier in the day to the Methodist church by my lake house. I'd driven past it a million times, but I'd never gone inside. Since I'd fallen asleep before finishing Genesis, I felt like I needed a quick tutorial on God. That's why I decided to stop by: to pick the brain of the church's pastor.

When I walked through the front door, the secretary behind the front desk smiled at me.

"Can I help you?" she asked.

"Hi, I don't go to this church, but I'm interested in learning more about God. Is your pastor available to talk for a few minutes?"

"Certainly. If you want to find a seat in the sanctuary, I'll send in our pastor. Who should I say is here?"

"My name is Christian. Christian Hagios."

She gestured toward the sanctuary to my left. As I headed that way, she picked up the phone and called the pastor. The doors were open, so I walked in and sat in a wooden pew near the back. I looked up at the stained-glass windows on either side of the sanctuary. The sunlight caused the colored glass to glow. I noticed all kinds of Biblical scenes within the glass. Noah and the ark. Moses parting the Red Sea. David killing Goliath. Jesus healing the sick. The red, blue, yellow, green, and orange stained glass mesmerized me.

I then turned my attention to the front of the sanctuary. A large wooden cross hung from the ceiling. Behind it, a massive stained-glass window showed Jesus in white robes rising up to the heavens. It was a beautiful work of art. Serenity filled my soul. I felt a sense of peace. I didn't realize being in church could calm my nerves and help me feel so safe and secure.

I heard footsteps coming toward me, so I stood and turned to greet the pastor. To my surprise, the pastor was a woman. I reached out my hand and introduced myself. She smiled warmly and grabbed my hand. She was tall and plain-looking with short brown hair and warm blue eyes. She didn't look like a pastor. Instead of wearing a white robe, she wore a red sweater and black pants.

"It's nice to meet you, Christian. I'm Pastor Laura Niles. How can I help you?"

I scooted down so we could sit together in the same pew. I wanted to come right out and tell her about my guardian angel, about how I'm supposed to save the world, but I also didn't want to come across as a crazy person. I took a different tact.

"I have a lake house right down the street," I began. "I've driven past your church countless times, and I'm thinking about coming to service this Sunday."

"Great," Laura said with a smile. "We'd love to have you."

"Something happened to me recently and I'm hoping you can help me make sense of it."

"I'll certainly try," she said.

"By the way, I love your church. It's really peaceful in here."

"Thank you. That's what we were going for when we designed this sanctuary. Life is so hard and messy and stressful and sad, so we created a place where people can leave their troubles at the door and find a sense of peace. What seems to be troubling you today, Christian?"

I decided to come right out with it. "Are there such things as guardian angels?"

Laura leaned back and smiled. "Oh, wow. You're diving right in, aren't you. I'll tell you, there is a difference of opinion when it comes to the existence of guardian angels. Some believe they exist. Others don't."

"What do you believe?"

"Me? I'd like to believe we all have a guardian angel looking over us. It brings me comfort to think that an angel from heaven is by my side, guiding me through this life. We certainly see many examples of angels in the Bible. When I think of guardian angels, I think of Daniel, how an angel protected him after he was thrown into the lion's den. Or how an angel protected Shadrach, Meshach and Abednego when King Nebuchadnezzar threw them into the fiery furnace. There are other examples, like how an angel spoke to both Joseph and Mary before Jesus' birth; how an angel warned Lot not to look back when he and his family escaped Sodom; how an angel freed Peter from his chains in prison. There are many more examples I can share."

"So, are you saying guardian angels are real?" I asked.

"No one know for sure, but Psalm 91:11 reads, 'For He will give His angels orders concerning you, to protect you in all your ways.' The Bible acknowledges that God sends angels to earth to protect His people."

"What if I told you my guardian angel visited me?" I asked, holding my breath, afraid of her reaction. Would Pastor Laura call me crazy and kick me out of her church? "Would you think I'm crazy?"

Pastor Laura leaned back in the pew and exhaled loudly. She crossed her legs and pursed her lips. I could tell she suddenly worried about my sanity. "Okay, tell me about it."

"What I'm about to tell you will sound crazy, but I swear all of it is true. Last night, my guardian angel appeared before me in human form. He said his name is Mike..."

"Mike?" Pastor Laura asked. "As in Michael, the Archangel?"

"Archangel? What is that?"

"One of the most well-known and most powerful angels in the Bible is Michael. Michael is the leader of all angels and archangels. He's known as the chief prince of heaven. He is the only angel mentioned by name in the Bible, the Torah, and the Quran. He's typically associated with the apocalypse."

"That makes sense," I muttered.

"What do you mean?" Pastor Laura asked.

"Mike told me that God chose me to save all of humanity."

"I'm sorry, what?"

"I know it sounds crazy. I'm still struggling to process it all myself. But Mike, I mean, Michael the Archangel, said God chose me before I was born to save the world."

Laura sat up straight. "Okay, you seem to be a very sane and reasonable man. Are you telling me that Michael actually came down from heaven to talk to you? Or do you think maybe all of this happened to you in a dream?"

Not wanting to freak her out, I decided to play along. "Yes, you're right, it was a dream. Didn't I say that at the start? Sorry. Yes, it was a dream. I'm wondering if it means anything."

"God does speak to us through our dreams," Pastor Laura said with a smile, relieved, "but often times, dreams mean nothing. They are just a collection of random thoughts and images. What do you do for a living, Christian?"

I felt like she was probing my mental state to determine if she was in danger and should call police. "I'm a writer for National Geographic."

"You work for National Geographic?" Laura asked, impressed. "How long have you worked for them?"

"About 25 years. My wife is a photographer for them. They hired both of us right out of college. We've been lucky to travel the world and share stories about all kinds of interesting things. In fact, I'm thinking about going to the Holy Land and writing an article about angels." I lied, hoping she wouldn't think I'm crazy.

"Now it all makes sense," she said. "No wonder you're dreaming about angels."

"That must be it," I say.

"Actually, I did my seminary thesis on angels."

"You did? Then, I obviously came to the right place," I said.

"What else do you want to know?"

"Do you know if an angel has visited anyone since the Bible came out? Maybe recently?"

Pastor Laura laughed. "Some people have claimed to have been visited by angels, but it's hard to prove. Is it an actual angel or a hallucination?"

"Or a dream," I add.

"Exactly. But honestly, if someone believes an angel visited them and it deepens their faith or brings them comfort, then where's the harm in that? Maybe angels are visiting people. Who am I to say? Any other questions?"

"Not that I can think of."

Pastor Laura stood. "Will you follow me?" She led me out the far side of the pew back to the front desk. She grabbed a card with her name and phone number on it and handed it to me. "If you have any other questions, feel free to call me. Anytime. Hopefully I helped you a little bit?"

"You did," I said as I grabbed her card. "Thank you."

I come out of my daze and see Anna walking through the front door. I stand up and walk around the table as she approaches. She lets me hug her but doesn't kiss me. I steel myself for the conversation ahead. I say a silent prayer to God and Mike, hoping she will forgive me so we can move forward, together.

CHAPTER 8

The doorbell awakens me from my slumber. I open my eyes and see Anna's beautiful face next to mine. She looks peaceful. Her eyes are closed. She breathes softly, still asleep. I wipe the gunk from my eyes, roll over, and look at my watch. It's nearly 8:30 a.m. I think about our conversation the previous night at Jasper's. I'm so grateful she forgave me and let me go home with her. I smile thinking about the intimate moments we shared after dinner. It renewed our love and solidified our intentions to repair our marriage.

The doorbell rings again and Anna stirs.

"Are you going to get that?" she asks without opening her eyes.

I sit up on my elbow and softly caress her long hair. "Yup, I'll get it." I kiss her cheek and roll out of bed.

I'm wearing shorts and a T-shirt. I walk downstairs to answer the door and through the side glass window, I see Mike. He catches my eye and waves. I open the door to greet him. I'm excited to see him again. Might he be here to tell me what God has planned for me? I'm also excited for Anna to meet him. I could see doubt in her eyes when I told her about Mike being my guardian angel.

"You truly don't expect me to believe your guardian angel visited you in human form, do you?" she asked me at dinner.

"I swear! I know it sounds crazy, but it's true," I answered.

Now here was Mike, my guardian angel, standing on my front porch, holding two cups of coffee. He wore a different outfit from the last time I saw him: jogging pants and a hoodie with a script on the front that read, 'I'm 99% angel, but oh, that 1%.'

"Funny," I said as I pointed to his sweatshirt.

"I thought I'd lighten the mood."

"Why so casual?"

"Why not?" he answers as he walks inside. "I want to be comfortable when I'm in my human form. Here." He hands me one of the coffees. "Cream and sugar, just as you like it."

"Thank you," I say.

"This is for Anna," Mike says. "Black, just as she likes it."

"Why did you ring the doorbell? You could've just appeared out of thin air."

"When I'm human, I like to do human stuff. For instance, I could have conjured up your coffee out of thin air, but instead I went to Black Dog Coffee and ordered it in person."

"How'd you get here?"

"I walked."

"Why are you here?" I ask.

"We have a lot of things to talk about."

"Chris, who is it?" Anna calls from the bedroom.

"It's Mike, my guardian angel," I yell back up in a cheery tone.

"Very funny," she yells back down.

"I'm not kidding," I say. "Come on down and meet him."

"Do you mind if I have another Twinkie?" Mike asks. "I know you have a box in the kitchen."

"It's so weird, having you know things about me."

"I know everything," Mike says with a wink.

I lead the way to the kitchen. I go to the box of Twinkies on the counter, pull one out, and give it to Mike. He sets Anna's coffee on the counter, opens up the Twinkie, and stuffs the whole thing in his mouth.

"Hungry?" I ask, laughing, as I take a sip of my coffee.

Mike chews the cream-filled sponge cake, swallows, and asks, "Can you get me a glass?"

"Sure" I say, thinking he wants some water to wash down the Twinkie. "Water?" I ask as I walk to the refrigerator.

"No, just bring me the glass please."

I shrug and walk it over to him. As Mike holds the glass, his hand glows. To my astonishment, water appears at the bottom of the glass and rises to the top.

"Wow! How'd you do that?" I ask.

"Magic," Mike says. He hands me the glass. "Drink. This is not just ordinary water. This is living water. The Holy Spirit is in this water."

"You want me to drink the Holy Spirit?"

Mike nods. "It will help you do God's work."

It tastes like ordinary water, but after I finish, I feel a strange warmth emanate throughout my entire being. I wonder how having the Holy Spirit inside me will help.

Anna walks into the kitchen Mike turns to her and says, "Hi, Anna. I'm Mike. I brought you some coffee."

"Thank you," Anna says as she picks up her coffee. She reads the label on the side of the paper cup. "Black Dog? Mmm, my favorite."

"I know," Mike says.

I place the glass on the marble countertop. I suddenly feel strong. Confident. Ready. "Something's happening to me," I say.

"Chris tells me you're an angel," Anna blurts out.

Mike smiles warmly. He addresses Anna first. "Yes, I'm an angel. Christian's guardian angel. I know he told you last night and you doubted him, but he speaks the truth. God has a very important mission for Christian. But to complete this mission, he'll need your love and support." Mike then turns to me. "That warmth you feel is the Holy Spirit filling your entire being."

"You expect me to believe you're an angel?" Anna asks.

A warm white light suddenly surrounds Mike's body. He becomes translucent, and his being sparkles. Like glitter. Soft, white wings of white energy stretch out from his back, and he floats up off the ground. Anna drops her coffee in shock. She steps by my side and both our mouths drop open as Mike floats above us. After a few seconds, he returns to the ground. His wings retract, and the light disappears.

"I... can't... believe what I just saw," Anna says with awe. "I am so sorry I doubted you."

"Why didn't you do that when I doubted you?" I ask.

Mike laughs. "I'm not supposed to show my true angel self to humans, but our time here is running short. I thought it better to reveal myself now rather than spend the next hour trying to convince you."

"Oh, I'm convinced," Anna says with reverence on her face.

"Me, too," I say. Any doubts I had before are now completely gone. "So, tell me more about this magical water. Can Anna have some?"

"I'm sorry, but it's just for you, since you've been assigned to be God's prophet."

"So, you weren't kidding," Anna says to me as she picks her coffee cup up off the floor. I grab a paper towel, mop up her spilled coffee, and throw it in the trash can.

"You're going to need God's guidance for the road ahead. The Holy Spirit will give you clarity. The Holy Spirit will lead you and help you do and say the right things. It will give you the wisdom and authority you need, so people will listen. Think of it as a way for God to reach others."

"Will God take control of my mind and body?"

Mike shakes his head and continues to smile, amused with my naivete. "No, you'll still have free will. But if you lean into the Holy Spirit and ask for guidance, it will reveal in your mind the right path."

"Okay," I say with apprehension. I try it. I silently ask the Holy Spirit what I should do next. The answer forms in my head, and my gut tells me what to say. "The Holy Spirit is telling me we need to go in the living room and sit down so you can tell me my purpose."

"I can tell you your purpose right now," Mike says.

I grab Anna's arm and lean into her, excited to finally learn what God wants from me.

"God wants you and Anna to recover the Ark of the Covenant."

CHAPTER 9

"The what?" I ask, confused.

"The Ark of the Covenant," Anna repeats. She looks at Mike. "But that's been missing for 2500 years." Anna knows more about biblical history than me since she grew up going to church.

"Isn't that the thing Indiana Jones found in 'Raiders of the Lost Ark'?" I ask.

"It is," Mike says. "Let's go in the next room so we can discuss this further."

We walk into the living room. Mike sits in the recliner while Anna and I sit next to each other on the sofa, right across from Mike.

Mike smiles and says, "I'm so glad you two made up last night."

"Me, too," I answer. "I still have a lot of groveling to do, but I think we're on the right track."

"We are," Anna confirms as she grabs my hand and squeezes.

"Marriage is hard. But it's so worth fighting for. Especially when two people love each other, like you two. I know life hasn't been easy since Henry took his own life."

Anna gasps, lets go of my hand, and covers her face. I look over and see she is crying.

"Coming to terms with the loss of a loved one is probably the hardest thing a person has to do during their lifetime," Mike says. "You miss them and often struggle to resume life without them. If only people understood how after death, they are reunited with their loved ones."

"I don't understand why my son took his own life," Anna cries.

Mike sits on the edge of the chair and puts his hands under his chin. He looks at Anna with sympathy. "Henry made a choice, Anna. I've talked to him in heaven, and he regrets it very much."

"Did Henry have a guardian angel?" Anna asks.

"He did."

"Then why didn't his guardian angel stop him from killing himself?"

"As I told Christian, a guardian angel's job is not to control their soul's life but to walk by their side and lead them in the right direction."

"Does everyone have a guardian angel?" Anna asks.

"Yes, plus guide angels."

"Guide angels?" I ask.

"Think of guide angels as young angels learning on the job," Mike explains. "Your guide angels help you find your calling. Every single soul is assigned between three to eight guide angels, who are all in different stages of angel evolution. They are learning on the job how to become guardian angels. Eventually, they get promoted to guardian angel."

"Interesting," Anna says with a look of confusion on her face.

"Let me explain it this way. Imagine you're in a room being interviewed by police. The main interrogator is in the room with you while the other cops are listening behind the mirror. Think of your guardian angel as the interrogator, while your guide angels are the cops behind the mirror. They're listening and taking notes and learning. They can come into the room at any time to help, which they sometimes do, as all your angels work together to protect you and help you reach your full potential."

"Well, they did a shitty job protecting my son," Anna says as she wipes a tear from her cheek.

"Anna, I promise you, Henry's angels tried to lead him away from suicide, but in the end, Henry was determined to leave this world. Every soul has a say in when they want to leave this world, and Henry decided it was his time. It's not your fault he left early. Just know he loved you both very much."

"I've had dreams of him since his death," Anna says.

"That's how he visits you," Mike says.

"In my dreams?"

"Yes, souls have an opportunity after death to visit their loved ones in their dreams, to let them know they're all right. Tell me your dream."

"I dreamt I was at our lake house when Henry walked into the room. I started crying and ran over to hug him. He asked me why I was crying, and I told him I missed him. He then said not to cry, that he was right here with me. And then I woke up."

"Interesting," Mike says. "You can't see him, but Henry does visit you often. In fact, he's here right now."

"He is?" Anna gasps.

"Yes. Do you want to see him?"

Anna looks up at Mike. "Right now?"

"How?" I ask.

Mike raises his arm toward the fireplace. A beam of light shoots out of his hand and in the light, Henry appears. His being glitters with white light. He smiles at us.

"Oh, Henry," I cry out toward him, wishing I could hold him again.

"Henry!" Anna yells with excitement. "I miss you so much!"

'I miss you, too, mom and dad,' I hear him say in my mind, though his mouth doesn't move.

Henry looks at me, then at Anna. His smile conveys a sense of peace and happiness. He waves at us and in my mind, I hear him say, 'I'm so sorry for what I did. I love you.'

"I love you, too, son," I say aloud.

"I love you, Henry," Anna says. It appears we can both hear him.

'Don't be sad,' Henry says. 'It's not your fault I ended my life early. Listen to Michael and live your life. Try to find happiness again, for me. I'm so glad you two are back together. I'll see you again when your time comes.'

The light fades and Henry disappears. Mike lowers his right arm.

"Don't go," Anna cries. She stands up and takes two quick steps to where Henry had stood. She turns to Mike. "Can you bring him back?"

"I'm sorry, but no," Mike replies. "I only let you see him to set your hearts at ease. You have an important job ahead of you and I need you to focus."

"But, where did Henry go?" Anna asks.

"Back to the spirit world," Mike says. "He's still here. You just can't see him. There is a veil between this world and heaven. Hopefully, seeing Henry again will help you overcome your sadness so you can focus on the task at hand."

"You mean, finding the Ark of the Covenant?" I ask.

"Exactly," Mike says.

Anna walks back to the couch, sits beside me, wipes her tears, and grabs my hand. She squeezes it tightly.

"Okay," Anna says calmly. "What do you need us to do?"

"We're going to fly to Jordan in two days and recover God's Ark of the Covenant. We'll bring it back here."

"But isn't that dangerous?" I ask. "In 'Raiders of the Lost Ark,' when they opened it, everyone's face melted."

Mike laughs. "That was just a movie. I promise, your face will not melt after you open it."

"Why does God want us to find it?" I ask.

"It's time. It's been hidden inside Mount Ebo for 2500 years. God wants to do something so big, His people will be inspired to become faithful and go back to believing in His existence."

"You want me to go with you?" Anna asks.

"Yes, and bring your camera. You'll be taking pictures for National Geographic."

"Really?" she asks.

"Yes, the magazine has a wide reach. An article on the discovery of the Ark of the Covenant will reach millions of people all over the world."

“But our boss doesn’t know we’re going. It takes months to get a story approved and on the printing schedule,” I argue. “Plus, it typically takes a few weeks to organize a trip like this.”

“Oh, ye of little faith,” Mike says. “May I see your phone?”

I reach into my pocket and pull out my cell phone. I hand it to Mike. He opens the home screen and presses a phone number. He turns it on speaker so we can hear. A familiar voice answers.

“Christian! It’s been a while. Hey, first of all, I’m sorry about your son. Did you and Anna get the flowers and card we sent?”

“We did,” Mike says in my voice. He sounds exactly like me! Anna squeezes my hand and smiles. I am astonished. “Thank you, Jim. By the way, Anna and I are ready to head out into the field again.”

“Great!” my boss says. “I don’t have anything available right now, but I will. . . .”

“I actually have a story for you,” Mike says, still with my voice. “I know the location of the Ark of the Covenant.”

“THE Ark of the Covenant? From the Bible?”

“The very one,” Mike continues. “A friend of mine invented a very powerful X-ray machine and found it hidden in a cave in Mount Ebo in Jordan. I’d like to get my regular crew together plus a religious expert and go find it. How's your budget looking?"

"Wow, the Ark of the Covenant," my boss says. "How sure are you about this information? I can't finance this trip on a hunch."

"I have an X-ray picture of it," Mike says. "I can send it over to you this afternoon."

'A picture?' I mouth to Anna. She shrugs.

"We only need three days – two days to fly there and one day to find it. If Mary can book our flights, we'll leave Tuesday and be back by Friday. I can send over the names in my group this afternoon."

"How many will be flying to Jordan?"

"Six of us, total. The standard. I promise you will not regret this."

There is a long pause as Jim thinks about it.

"I'll want to send a camera crew as well, so we can air this discovery on our Nat Geo channel."

"Of course! But it needs to be small for this trip. Just a photographer and producer."

"No problem. I'll send Eli and Marcus."

"Perfect. I love working with them. Can you have them meet us at the Queen Alia International Airport in Jordan this Tuesday afternoon?"

"Two days from now? Those airline tickets are going to be costly, Chris."

"I know," Mike says with my voice. "I promise you won't regret it. National Geographic will own exclusive rights to this discovery. You'll make a fortune on magazine sales and video rights to other networks."

"What about the Jordanian government? They're not going to let you take the Ark out of their country, will they?"

"I've already spoken to the Director of Antiquities and cut him a deal."

"A deal? What kind of deal… " Jim says with a sense of dread in his voice.

"It includes the Smithsonian, once we recover the Ark. First, Jermaine will take it to his lab in Lawrence, Kansas, to confirm its authenticity, which he will, since it's the real Ark. Then, Jermaine will arrange to ship it to Washington D.C. The Smithsonian will pay the Jordanian government a million dollars a year for the next twenty years for the right to display the Ark inside one of its museums."

"A million dollars a year? That seems like a steal for the Smithsonian," Jim says. "They could make that in a week by charging admission."

"But they won't. They'll keep the admission into the museum free. They have the budget and donors ready to finance it once we deliver the goods. Honestly, the Jordanian Director of Antiquities laughed in my face when I told him we were going to recover the Ark of the Covenant inside Mount Ebo. He doesn't think it's really there, which is why he agreed to this deal. Plus, the chance to funnel a million dollars a year into his country was too much to resist. So, I got him to sign the contract."

"Great! Please send me a copy of that along with the X-ray image of the Ark."

"I will as soon as we get off the phone."

Jim sighs. "Chris, this trip will drain my travel budget for the rest of the year. I need you to come through for me."

"I will. I promise it's there. And again, once we publish this story, Jim, there will be so much money coming back at you, you'll be able to finance ten more trips this year."

"All right, please don't make me regret this."

"I won't. Thanks, Jim. I'll call you when we return." Mike hangs up the phone.

"Wow," is all I can say.

"You sounded just like Chris!" Anna exclaims.

"I've been listening to him talk his whole life," Mike says.

"It's so weird knowing you've been by my side, spying on me my entire life."

"Spying?" Mike asks.

"That's what it is," I say. "But spying in a good way. I mean, you did save my life a few times."

"987 times," Mike says with a smile.

"987 times?" Anna asks.

"I'll explain later," I say. "By the way, who are the other three people going with us?"

"Your friends Adom and Jermaine."

"Great!" I say.

"And Pastor Laura."

"Who's Pastor Laura?" Anna asks.

"A pastor at the church by our lake house. I stopped and picked her brain yesterday."

"He was struggling to believe I'm an angel," Mike says. "She will be the religious expert for your article."

"How will I convince her to go with us?" I ask. "I barely know her."

"I already took care of it," Mike says. "She's in. I also called Adom and Jermaine. They will all be at your house tonight to discuss the trip."

"Tonight?"

"We don't have a lot of time to plan. We need supplies, food rations, and some other things."

"Mike, can I ask you a question?" Anna asks.

"Sure."

"Are you my guardian angel, too?" Anna asks.

"No, you have your own guardian angel. Her name is Angelina. You can't see her, but she's here right now, right by your side, guiding you. God assigns every soul a guardian angel before they are sent to earth. Then, after you're born, we stay by your side for the duration of your life. You can't see us - though I am breaking that rule with both of you. With God's permission, of course. But again, our job is to lead you to the good path."

"What's the good path?" Anna asks.

"The one that leads you closer to God."

"Is there a bad path," I ask.

"Yes," answers Mike. "Any choice that leads you away from God. This world is filled with demons. Satan's minions. They are constantly trying to get people to turn their back to God."

"So, Satan is real?" Anna asks.

"Oh, yes, only his real name is Lucifer. He's a fallen angel. He used to be my friend..." Mike trails off. "Lucifer went against God, so God exiled him to earth. He and his demons are constantly trying to undermine God by tempting His souls to do bad things. And when people fall under Lucifer's spell, they struggle to find their way back to God. But hopefully, as God's prophet, you can open people's eyes to the beauty of God's love and grace."

"No pressure," I joke.

Mike isn't smiling. "All kidding aside, you have your hands full, Christian. First, you need to recover the Ark of the Covenant. Then, you'll need to save the world."

CHAPTER 10

Anna and I sit at our kitchen table with everyone going on this trip. I look around and smile at Pastor Laura, who sits directly to my left. I can tell she's excited for this adventure. She doesn't know us well but has quickly acclimated herself to our group. She is extremely friendly and bright and will serve as the religious expert for my article. Next to her sits Jermaine, my old college friend who is currently a professor of anthropology at the University of Kansas. He has access to a lab where he can run tests to confirm the authenticity of archaic objects. When we bring the Ark back to Kansas City, he will take it to Lawrence and run an elemental analysis to confirm the makeup of the Ark of the Covenant. He will also use an electron microscope to date it. Next to Jermaine sits Adom, our guide. He has men all over the world who help him with archeological digs. He will have a group of men waiting for us in Jordan to drive us to Mount Ebo. Next to Adom sits Mike, who watches us as we talk. Since Laura and Jermaine live close, they drove into Kansas City that night. Adom flew in from New York and just arrived after a long day in the sky. He looks tired.

The excitement in the room is palpable as Mike explains our mission.

"Thank you all for coming," Mike begins. "My name is Mike, and I'm the one who found the Ark of the Covenant."

"Christian tells me you found it in Mount Ebo in Jordan," Jermaine says. "How did you find it?"

"My team in Texas built a supersonic X-ray machine," Mike lies. Mike was the first one to arrive at my house that night, and he told Anna and I right away that he planned to lie to my friends. He said it was necessary. He doesn't want them to discover his true identity as an angel, so he urged Anna and I to go along with his fabricated story. We agreed. I mean, when an angel asks you to do something, you do it. Right? "The X-ray machine my team built can see through thick walls of rock and sediment. We flew to Mount Ebo in Jordan last week, powered it up, and found the Ark hidden behind a wall of rock." He passes out pictures of the X-ray showing the Ark. I still don't know how he created the picture, but then I know angels have powers I can't even begin to understand. Everyone looks down at the pictures of the Ark in awe. "As you can see from this X-ray, there is no doubt about it. It's the Ark of the Covenant. We couldn't get to it because rock and mud have sealed the cave entrance. That's why I'm taking all of you with me to recover it. We'll need dynamite to blow it up. That's where you come in, Adom."

Adom nods.

"I've marked the entrance, so I know exactly where it is. We won't need to bring my cumbersome machine, thank goodness. It's a pain to lug around. The plan is to leave the day after tomorrow. So, tomorrow, let's go shopping for supplies. Then, when we arrive in Jordan on Tuesday, plan on sleeping outside for a couple nights. We'll need to buy tents, sleeping bags, water bottles, and hiking shoes. The usual gear. I know most of you are all well-versed in expeditions like this one, so get what you need." Mike pulls out a credit card from his pocket and holds it up. "I have a pretty big budget for this trip, so it's all on me. Plus, National Geographic is chipping in, too."

Mike then reaches into his back pocket and pulls out hotel key cards.

"I've also booked all of you rooms at the hotel down the street."

I smile, remembering my conversation with Mike earlier that night when he mentioned that he planned to pay for hotel rooms and supplies.

"I didn't know angels had money," I said.

"We don't."

"Then how do you get money? Do you have a bank account, or do you use cash?"

Mike waved his hands and a credit card appeared. "I use a credit card."

"How does an angel get approved for a credit card?" I laughed.

"You underestimate my powers, Christian. God's powers. What is money and a bank account but numbers on a computer screen? It's easy for me to manipulate technology to create digital currency. I don't need gold coins, like I did the last time I came to earth in human form. I can simply conjure up a bank account with money in it and then use a credit card to buy things. The bank is none the wiser."

"You make it sound so easy," I said.

"It is. For me. Remember, God and angels can do things you can't even fathom."

I smile, remembering our conversation and return my focus to Mike as he continues explaining the details of our journey ahead. "Before we set out on this quest together as a fellowship…"

"The Fellowship of the Ark," I joke, and everyone laughs.

"I want to tell you all about the Ark of the Covenant," Mike continues. "Just so we are all on the same page.

"In the year 2015 B.C., God commanded Moses to build an Ark while he and his people were camped at the base of Mount

Sinai. God chose a skilled craftsman by the name of Bezalel to build it. Bezalel built the Ark, per God's detailed instructions, using acacia wood. He then plated it with gold, both inside and out. The lid to this golden box, also called the Mercy Seat, contains two Cherubs made of pure gold. The Cherubs face each other with their wings wrapped around their bodies. There are four gold rings attached to either side of the box with two golden poles resting inside the rings. The poles make it easy to carry the Ark from place to place.

"As some of you know from the Bible, God gave Moses the Ten Commandments on Mount Sinai, but when he came down, he saw his people worshipping a golden calf. Filled with rage, Moses threw the stone tablets to the ground, breaking them into pieces. Those pieces of the original Ten Commandments are inside the Ark. So, too, are the second set of the Ten Commandments which Moses carved later. Those tablets are still in one piece. Moses also put a gold jar of manna inside the Ark along with Aaron's staff. God placed great powers inside Aaron's staff, and Aaron used his staff to conjure up the first two plagues on Egypt: Turning water to blood and calling the frogs from the water.

"As for the Ark, it is considered a manifestation of God's physical presence on earth. When God spoke to Moses in the tent in the desert, he did so from between the two Cherubs on the

Mercy Seat. In the days after Moses death, as the Jews moved the Ark from city to city, many who looked at it or touched it died. Eventually, King David moved the Ark to the Temple in Jerusalem. When the Babylonians attacked Jerusalem in 586 B.C., the Ark disappeared. Since then, many have tried to find it but have failed.

"There are many theories as to where it is hidden. One of the most fascinating stories comes out of Ethiopia. They claim to have the Ark inside the Church of Saint Mary of Zion in Axum, Ethiopia, guarded by a monk known as the 'Keeper of the Ark'. They claim to have acquired it during the reign of Solomon. They say his son, Menelik, stole the Ark after a visit to Jerusalem and brought it there. I tell you; this claim is false. The Ark is not in Ethiopia.

"Others believe the Ark never left Jerusalem. Some say it is still hidden underneath the Temple Mount. As the story goes, in 586 B.C, the king of Jerusalem at the time, Josiah, received a warning that the Babylonians were about to attack. Worried about the fate of the Ark, Josiah had his men dig a hole under a wooden storehouse on the Temple Mount, and they supposedly buried the Ark there. One archaeologist claims he's found the exact spot where the Holy of Holies is located – in a section of bedrock cut in the dimensions matching those of the Ark. This archeologist believes the Ark is buried deep inside the Temple Mount. But he is also wrong.

"As you can see from the X-ray in front of you, the Ark is actually sealed up in cave in Mount Nebo in Jordan. How did it get there, you ask? Let me tell you. Back in 586 B.C., as the Babylonians headed to Jerusalem to destroy the Temple, God told the prophet Jeremiah to take the Ark out of Jerusalem and hide it in a cave in Mount Nebo. He and his followers carried it across the River Jordan and delivered it into one of the many caves within the mountain. This is the same mountain where Moses gazed out upon the Promised Land before he died. God then sealed up the entrance so no one would ever find it. However, thanks to modern technology, my team has been able to find its exact location inside Mount Nebo. And thanks to National Geographic and my successful business in Texas, we have the funding to go to Jordan and recover the Ark of the Covenant."

"That's fascinating," Jermaine says. "I'm sorry, but how do you know Christian? I've known him since college, and he's never mentioned you."

"I am a big fan of his articles in National Geographic. When I found the location of the Ark, I knew right away this was a story that needs to be shared with the world. And who better to share that then my favorite writer, Christian Hagios."

I smile at Jermaine and nod.

“So,” Mike continues. “I called up National Geographic, told them about my discovery, and requested I work with Christian. So, our friendship is fairly new.”

“Mike’s right,” I say to reinforce his lie. “We just met last week.”

Adom raises his hand. “Do we have permission from the Jordanian government to go into the mountain?”

“Yes, that’s already been arranged and should not be a problem,” Mike says.

“How exciting!” Laura says. “If you’re right about the Ark, we’re about to make the greatest discovery in more than two thousand years.”

“Prepare yourselves, friends,” Mike says. “After we recover the Ark, your lives will be changed forever. Everyone in the world will know your name. This discovery will change the way everyone thinks about God and help bring all of humanity closer to Him. My hope is it will make believers out of nonbelievers, that people will become kinder and more generous. I believe it will change the world for the better.”

“Another question, Mr. Mike.” Adom says.

“Yes, Adom,” Mike says.

"Actually, I have two. One, how do we know we won't die after we find the Ark? You just said that many who looked at the Ark died."

"There is no guarantee," Mike says. "Going on this trip will be a risk. But if it calms your nerves, know that I will be the first one in the cave. I will take that risk for the group. That way, if I die, you can quickly re-seal the cave and leave the Ark behind. Next question?"

"If you don't die after we find it, how will we get the Ark back here, to Kansas City?"

"I've already taken care of those arrangements," Mike says. "Don't stress about a thing. After we find the Ark, all will be revealed."

CHAPTER 11

I sit next to Mike in a large, comfortable airline seat. Anna is on the other side of him, sitting by the window. We're not in first-class but also not economy. Adom, Jermaine, and Pastor Laura sit in the back of the plane. Anna, Mike and I sit near the front.

"Why aren't we all sitting together?" I ask.

"I want to be able to talk to you both freely," Mike says as he buckles his seatbelt. "I appreciate you not letting them know I'm your guardian angel. It would just complicate things."

"Are you sure you're okay with the middle seat?" I ask.

"Do you want it?"

"Not really."

"Then don't worry. I'll get by."

"Do you like being human?" Anna asks. We speak in hushed tones so the people near us won't hear.

"Sure. It's a change of pace," Mike says. "However, I will say it's much easier being an angel than being a human. Being trapped inside this body, stuck inside this shell, where you feel pain, hunger, cold, those kinds of things? Not fun. However, just know when your soul leaves your body and goes to heaven, you won't have to worry about suffering anymore. We angels certainly don't suffer."

"Let me get this straight," I say. "You're an archangel, right? What is an archangel? And how is that different from a regular angel?"

"Great question," Mike says. "Archangels are God's original angels. It's Gabriel, Raphael, Uriel, Selaphiel, Jegudiel, Barachiel, Jeremiel and me. God created eight angels first, and then He tasked us with being His messengers. He also called on us to protect His souls from Lucifer and other demons.

"Most archangels have been angels longer than anyone else. Because of this, God puts us in a leadership position, and we work together to manage all the angels in heaven."

"Did you get demoted?" I ask. "Is that why you're my guardian angel?"

"I'm still an archangel," Mike explains. "But because you have such an important mission in this life, God trusted me to protect you. That's why I'm back to being a guardian angel. It's a one-time only situation. When you die and return to heaven, I'll go back to managing angels."

"Do you like your job?" I ask.

"I do! Being an archangel is a lot more fun than being a guardian angel."

"Why?" Anna asks.

"No offense, Christian, but looking after you is exhausting!"

"Gee, thanks," I say wryly.

"Guardian angels have to stay focused for the duration of a soul's life. Sure, guide angels can step in and help when a guardian angel needs a break, but the pressure is on the guardian to lead their soul in the right direction. When your assigned soul doesn't listen to their instinct and doesn't follow your guidance - when they do drugs, or sleep around, or hurt other people – it becomes a reflection on you as a guardian. If too many of your assigned souls stray away from God, you risk demotion. I've had to demote many a guardian angel whose souls gave in to the temptations laid out by Satan and his demons."

"What happens to a guardian angel if they get demoted?" I ask.

Mike opens his mouth to answer and then shuts it. "I can't answer that."

"Why not?" Anna asks.

"Because God wants me to stay vague when it comes to talking about life on the other side."

"Why?" Anna asks.

"Because the whole point of your human existence is to learn from adversity. If I tell you everything about life and heaven, I'll be cheating you out of the discovery process, which is so important for personal growth. God purposely created a harsh, brutal world with millions of challenges for you to navigate. But luckily for you two, this world is not nearly as brutal as it once was. You're so blessed. Think about the first humans. They couldn't go out to eat for dinner. They had to go into the wild and hunt for food. If they didn't find anything, they went hungry. They didn't have a nice house with central heating and indoor plumbing. They lived in caves and slept on rocks. Life was so much harder for them. But over the centuries, people have used their intellect to make life easier. Of course, you still face challenges. Just… different challenges. But regardless, at the end of the day, every soul should ask this question – are my decisions helping me grow closer to God or leading me further away from Him? Many blame God for their troubles, but that's when you should lean into Him. Those who lean into God will be rewarded in many ways, not only in this life but the next. God is always watching you. He wants His souls to grow in their faith through struggle."

"But struggling sucks," I say.

"Yes, it does," Mike laughs, "but struggle is necessary for growth. If God coddled you and gave you everything you needed all the time, you'd never learn. You'd never grow. You'd be stuck in a different type of purgatory. It is essential for all souls to experience uncertainty. If you already knew the answers, then what would be the point of living? How boring would life be if you already knew everything? God wants you to figure it all out on your own through experience. There is a beauty in overcoming struggle."

Our plane accelerates and soars into the sky. We are now airborne, heading toward the other side of the world.

"So, Mike," I ask, "let me get this straight. As my guardian angel, you've been with me every second of my life, right?"

"That's right."

"And you know everything about me. You always know what I'm doing, right?"

"That is correct," Mike answers.

"So why, if you saw me drowning at the lake when I was a kid, why did you wait for me to die before saving me? Why didn't you save me earlier? Or stop me from going into the lake at all?"

Mike fidgets in his chair and hesitates. "Actually, I wanted you to die. But just for a short while."

"Why?" I ask.

"Because I knew you didn't believe in God or heaven and I hoped a near-death experience would help you see the light, so to speak. But it didn't work."

"It did, for a spell," I say. "But my parents, as you know, don't believe in God. They think organized religion is dumb. And being a young kid, I gradually reverted back to their way of thinking."

"Their divorce certainly didn't help," Mike says.

"You're right. I was mad at them. Mad at the world. For some reason, I doubled down on my doubts about God and eventually stopped believing. Anna tried to get me to believe again by forcing me to go to church with her on occasion. But it didn't work."

"It might've worked if you'd gone to church with me more often," Anna says with a laugh. "But no. It took a guardian angel coming down from heaven to get you to believe in God." Anna looks at Mike. "By the way, I do have a question I'd like to ask you. Is God a man or a woman?"

Mike chuckles. "Another question I can't answer. But I can tell you this: God created gender to make it easy for every living thing in this world to multiply. God gave beauty to both the male and female gender, and they are both equal in His eyes. Unfortunately, over the course of history, men have used their physical strength to take power and control over women. But in God' eye, men and women are both beautiful. In heaven, there is no gender. Just souls. And angels. And God, who is above all of it."

"Is there life on other planets?" Anna asks next.

"Yeah, are aliens real?" I ask.

Mike sits back and laughs. "You aren't messing around with these questions, are you? This is another one I can't answer. But I will say this: God LOVED creating this world. To think He would spend all eternity watching this one world is pretty narrow thinking. I'm not confirming he's created life on other planets. I'm just saying, if He wanted to create new life somewhere else, He could. He did it once. He could do it again."

The plane suddenly shakes uncontrollably. It dips up and down, causing my stomach to go into knots. Some of the passengers start to moan audibly, worried the plane might suddenly crash. One of the overhead bins opens, and a bag falls out.

"What's going on?" I ask.

"I'll be right back," Mike says. He unbuckles his seatbelt and goes into the bathroom as the plane continues to shake. My stomach is tied in knots as the plane dips, banks, then dips again.

About a minute later, the shaking stops. Mike walks out of the bathroom and sits back down.

"Sorry about that. I needed to right the plane and didn't want people to see me disappear."

The captain gets on the microphone.

"I apologize for the sudden turbulence," he says. "We hit a flock of birds, but all seems to be fine right now. We won't need to turn back as the engines are in good working order. If we need to make an emergency landing, I will let you know, but for now we will continue on to Jordan. The rest of the ride should be smooth."

Mike looks at me. "There is an evil in this world that doesn't want you to find the Ark of the Covenant."

"Evil?" I ask.

Mike nods. "I'm afraid Lucifer and his demons are going to do everything they can to keep us away from the Ark. They steered the birds into the engine to try and bring our plane down. But that's why I am here. I fixed the engine and put a shield of white light over this plane to protect it from further harm."

I look out the window but don't see any white light.

"You can't see it, but Lucifer and his demons can. It will keep them away from this plane for the rest of the flight."

My heartbeat races. My blood rushes to my ears. I break out in a sweat.

Reading my mind, Mike says, "Don't worry. Remember, I'm your Guardian Angel. My job is to protect you. And I will. Lucifer cannot hurt you. Not with me here. Remember, God chose you and He will make sure you stay safe."

"But why did He choose me? I'm nobody."

"God likes to work through those who least expect it. Look at Jesus. He was a carpenter's son who grew up in poverty. God doesn't like to work His miracles through the powerful. He prefers to work through normal, everyday people. And that's you."

"So, I'm not special," I say, begging for a compliment. Mike complies.

"If you weren't special, I wouldn't be here," he says.

I reach into my carry-on bag under my seat and pull out the Bible.

"You finally decided to read the Bible. I'm proud of you," Mike says.

"I need to cram for this test," I say. "Unfortunately, I'm a slow reader. I'm still in Genesis."

"Go ahead and jump to the next chapter and read Exodus. It details Moses' life and the Ark of the Covenant."

"Okay," I say as I open the Bible to Exodus.

"Learn all you can and gather your strength," Mike says. "I'm afraid we'll have to face more challenges before we can uncover the Ark."

CHAPTER 12

Mike, Anna and I exit the plane and wait for Adom, Jermaine, and Laura to join us. I raise my arms and stretch my tired muscles. I yawn as other passengers walk past us. I struggled to sleep during the overnight flight, as did Anna.

After the rest of our group joins us, we begin walking toward baggage claim. I walk next to Adom and put my arm around his shoulder.

"How did you sleep?"

"Not well, my friend," he says with a frown. "I don't like those tiny seats. I wish Mr. Mike had upgraded all of us."

"Sorry about that," Mike says, "but National Geographic has us on a tight budget. I could only afford three partial upgrades."

"Since I am providing the supplies and labor, maybe I should've been one of the upgrades."

"You can have my seat on the way back," Mike says.

"Ha, ha. Don't tease. You know I go back to Egypt after this."

"If there's any money left over after we recover the Ark, I'll pay for an upgrade for your flight to Cairo."

"If that is the case, then we go to lunch at McDonald's and only order off Value Menu," Adom laughs.

"Actually, that sounds pretty good," Laura says. "I'm getting hungry."

"Does Jordan have a McDonald's?" Anna asks.

"Every country has a McDonald's," Mike says. "It's the one thing you can count on. Besides death and taxes."

"Can we go there before we go to Mount Nebo?" Laura asks. "I'm hungry."

"Of course," Mike says.

I turn my attention back to Adom. "Thank you for making your crew available for this."

"Of course, Mr. Christian," Adom says. "How can I say no to finding the Ark of the Covenant. If Mr. Mike is right, this will be the greatest discovery in the history of mankind."

"No question," I say. "Plus, showing the world proof of God's existence will draw more people to believe in God."

"Pffft," Adom says as he sticks out his tongue.

"What was that?" Anna asks.

"Believe in God? Nonsense. There is no God."

"You don't believe God came to earth and dwelt within the Ark? You don't believe God was on the Ark when He spoke to Moses?" Laura asks.

"No, I don't believe that happened. They are stories from a long time ago. The Ark is just an artifact. To think God is real is silly."

I shake my head and say, "Thinking there is no God is silly. Of course there's a God, a God who loves us. Uncovering the Ark of the Covenant, the place where God stayed while visiting earth, will help prove to people that God really does exist."

"Unless I see God, I won't believe." Adom says. "We live in a godless world where people hurt others for their own gain. Bad things always happen to good people. If God is real, why doesn't He protect us from bad things? Like your son's death. Where was God?"

I give him a sad smile. "I know God was with Henry when he took his own life. Henry made a choice. Just as I make a choice every day to trust and love and believe in God."

"Wow," says Jermaine, chiming in. "I remember you being an atheist when we were in college?"

"I was. But let's just say, I've seen the error of my ways," I answer. I feel the Holy Spirit take control of my tongue. "A wise friend told me when we experience hardship, it doesn't mean God's abandoned us. He's still there. He's just letting us figure it out on our own. We should lean on Him for hope and comfort when times get tough."

"Still," Adom says. "Unless I have proof of God, I will not believe."

"I used to think like you," Pastor Laura says, joining in on our conversation. "But then I died."

We all stop suddenly, annoying the people behind us who go around. "I'm sorry, what?" I ask.

"I was born with a heart condition and had a heart transplant at 18," she tells our group as we resume walking. "I flat lined on the operating table for a few minutes and had a near-death experience."

"What happened?" I ask.

"Just like they say, my soul left my body. I floated above my body. I saw a white light and went toward it. I ended up visiting an amazing place filled with new colors, new sounds, beautiful music. Everything glittered. It's hard to describe because it's unlike anything here on earth. The afterlife is a beautiful, peaceful place. I didn't want to leave. But then, I felt my soul being pulled away and soon, I was back inside my body."

"Wow," is all I can say as I eat up her every word. I look at Mike and he nods, confirming Laura's story.

"That's amazing," Anna says.

"Before my heart surgery, I doubted the existence of God. I thought we lived, we died, and that was it. But after visiting heaven, I realized I was wrong. God is real. Heaven is real. After my surgery, I vowed to spend the rest of my life sharing God's love with others. That's why I became a pastor. Life is a gift. A gift from God. And there is no greater gift than God's love. I know many times we feel alone, as if God doesn't care about us. Our souls are trapped inside flesh and blood, and our ability to understand our purpose is limited due to our physical and mental shortcomings. But I can tell you with full assurance, heaven exists. I know many people like you, Adom, who refuse to believe until they have proof. I deal with doubters all the time at my church. Do you know what I tell them?"

"What do you tell them, Miss Laura?" Adom asks.

"I tell them that some of the greatest scientists of our time believed in God. Einstein, Newton, Bacon, Copernicus. Do you know why they believed in God?" Laura asks.

Adom shakes his head.

"They believed in a higher power because they knew the odds of a planet like ours simply existing was infinitesimal. Do you know the odds of humans evolving from single-cell organisms? One in 700 quintillion. A quintillion is a billion trillion. I mean, the chance of us even being here at all is impossibly low! These famous, well-respected scientists knew a higher power HAD to exist, a God who created this world and all of us in it, because the chances that a cloud of dust exploded and led to our existence is, for all practical purposes, simply impossible."

We arrive at baggage claim and wait for our bags to come out of the chute. I see our camera crew sitting off to the side. Eli and Marcus wave and pick up their gear to join us.

"I hear what you say," Adom continues. "I like your story, but I don't know. I will think about it."

Mike puts his hand on Adom's shoulder. "It's okay to doubt the existence of God. All of us struggle with doubt. But just know God loves you whether you believe in Him or not. I promise you, when you die and your soul ascends to heaven, you will know the truth of God's love. You will know He exists. It can be hard to see that sometimes from our human perspective, but when our soul leaves this world, the truth is revealed."

"We'll see, Mr. Mike," Adom says. Then, changing the subject, he asks, "By the way, you say you know *exactly* where the Ark is?"

"Yes," Mike answers.

"Good. My men are expensive, so we need to make good time."

"We'll make good time," Mike says.

"Hey guys," Marcus says as he and Eli joins us. They both have packs filled with travel supplies on their back. Eli also carries a camera in a hard case and a tripod. Marcus carries a large blue bag filled with camera batteries, microphones, and other supplies.

"We can help carry your equipment up the mountain," Jermaine says.

"I wish," Eli says, "but the union won't allow it. We're stuck carrying all this gear."

"I won't tell anyone if you need help," Jermaine says.

"Thanks," replies Marcus. "So, we're going to find the Ark of the Covenant?"

I nod.

"I want to get some interviews on tape once we get to the mountain and again after we find it."

"Of course," I say. "Whatever you need."

"Use the restroom now if you need to," Mike says. "I can watch your equipment while you go."

All of us use the bathroom. When we return, we find our checked luggage at Mike's feet. While we were gone, our packs came out of the chute and Mike grabbed them. We grab our gear, put them on our backs, and head outside. It's a sunny, warm day. It's also busy as many travelers greet family and friends at the curb. I take a deep breath of fresh air and sigh. I love visiting new places. This is the first time I've ever been to Jordan. I notice palm trees growing all around us, welcoming visitors. I see three camouflage-colored jeeps parked nearby. A dark-skinned man standing next to the first jeep waves at us.

"Adom!" he yells.

"Samir!" Adom returns the greeting. He turns to us. "Miss Laura, Mr. Jermaine, you both come with me in first jeep. Mr.

Mike, Mr. Christian, and Miss Anna, you all get in second jeep. Mr. Eli and Mr. Marcus? You get in last jeep." He then turns to Samir. "We go to McDonald's first." Samir gives him a thumbs up.

The two men in our jeep grab our bags and put them in the back. Anna pulls out her camera before handing over her backpack. We climb in the back seat.

"I'll take pictures as we head to Mount Nebo," Anna says.

"Great idea. How long will it take to get there?" I ask Mike.

"From Queen Alia Airport? About an hour. It should be an easy drive."

I look at my watch. It's 3 p.m. We should have enough daylight to get to the base of the mountain and establish camp for the night. I assume we'll uncover the Ark tomorrow.

As if reading my mind, Mike says, "Once we get to Mount Nebo, we'll hike a short way and set up camp. I'll take you to the Ark at first light tomorrow."

"How hard will it be to get inside the cave?" I ask.

"There's more than 25-hundred years of rock covering the entrance," Micheal says. "It will take a powerful explosion to open it up. That's why Adom's men brought dynamite."

"Can't you just wave your hands and remove the rock?" I ask. "It would save us a lot of time."

"I could, but where's the fun in that?" Mike answers.

We leave the airport, and a short time later, we enter a McDonald's drive thru. I can't read the menu since it's in Arabic, so I have the driver order me a Big Mac value meal. Greasy food never tasted so good! It's the one thing you can count on from McDonald's. The food will taste the same in Amman, Jordan, as it will in Kansas City, Missouri. My stomach aches soon after I finish my meal. I lean forward and press my arms into my belly.

"Too greasy?" Mike smiles as he takes his last bite of Big Mac

"Yeah. Anna has me on this healthy diet eating salads and other vegetables. I don't eat fast food that often."

"I'm saving your life is what I'm doing," she says. "Eating fruits and vegetables will help you live longer."

"Listen to you wife. She's right," Mike says. "Remember, God made the Garden of Eden for man to eat the fruit, not kill and eat the animals He also created."

"I know, but chicken tastes good. Cow and pig taste good. Especially when smoked and topped with barbecue sauce."

"True, I'll admit that burger did taste good." Mike says as he licks his fingers. "But just because it tastes good doesn't mean it's good for you. Anna is right. God made fruits and vegetables so you could eat them and live longer, healthier lives. If everyone would adopt such a diet, there would be a lot fewer health problems in this world."

“Man, now I’m getting it from both of you. Fine, I’ll eat healthier. I promise.”

I turn and look out at the scenery as we drive away from the city. We cross a bridge spanning the Jordan River. There is not much to see as the empty land is filled with brown sandy dunes and gnarly bushes and trees. Mount Nebo stands tall in the distance, 11,000 feet high with snow covering its peaks.

“Is the entrance to the Ark high up the mountain?” I ask, wondering how much climbing is ahead of us.

“No,” Mike answers. “We’ll hike up the mountain a little but not far. It’s below the snow line.”

I breathe a sigh of relief.

Mike talks to the driver in Arabic. The driver then honks and passes the first jeep. He drives off road onto the dry, dusty land and steers the jeep toward the base of Mount Nebo. We bounce as the terrain gives the shocks a good workout. The other two jeeps fall in behind us. Mike continues to give our driver directions in Arabic as we near Mount Nebo. Our driver stops 100 yards from the base of the mountain.

“This is good.” Mike says. The driver puts the jeep in park, and we climb out. We stretch. The sun feels good on my face. It’s about 80-degrees with a faint breeze. I turn and scan the horizon behind us. My heart skips a beat as I see a convoy of military vehicles coming our way. Jordanian police. A police officer stands in the back of each jeep, manning a machine gun. They point their guns at us.

"Uh, Mike." I point to the convoy heading our way. "It's the police."

Mike touches my shoulder to ease my anxiety. "It's okay. Remember, I'm here to protect you," he says. He then faces the group and says, "Stay calm, everyone. I'll handle this. Just don't make any sudden moves."

Eli puts his camera on his shoulder and begins recording as five military jeeps fan out around us. It's a strategic decision to keep a gun on all of us. The officers standing behind the machine guns rest their hands on the trigger. I notice the officers in the passenger seats all have their hands on their sidearms. We are outmanned and have no recourse but to do what they say.

An officer with medals on his shirt steps out of one of the Jeeps and approaches. We put our hands up in the air to avoid a deadly confrontation. Micheal walks up to the captain and begins speaking in Arabic. The captain moves his arms up and down to get us to lower our arms. We comply. He talks to Mike for a few seconds. Mike pulls out a piece of folded paper from his back pocket and hands it to the captain. The captain opens it and looks at it. As he does, Mike pulls out a wad of cash from his front pocket and hands it to the captain. The captain smiles, takes the money, and stuffs it in his pocket. He then circles his hand in the air, shouts in Arabic, and the jeeps leave. I sigh in relief. This is not the first time a local government has tried to shut us down before we even started, but it's always a tense moment since there's no guarantee they'll give us permission to do our job.

"That was amazing" Jermaine says as he slaps Mike on the back. "The officers in these foreign countries can be such jerks. We've been arrested a couple times, haven't we, Christian?"

"We have. Remember the Honduras?"

"I do. And Columbia."

"Yeah, we tend to go into some pretty dangerous places," I say.

"That's where all the treasure is, for some odd reason," Jermaine answers.

Mike addresses all of us. "Let's leave the cars here. Grab our supplies and we'll begin our ascent. There is a bluff twenty minutes from here where we can make camp."

We grab our backpacks and prepare to hike. Anna starts snapping pictures of the scenery around us while Adom's crew grabs boxes of explosives.

We begin our ascent up Mount Nebo.

As we walk up a slope and turn a corner, I gaze up past the rocky hill of olive trees and look to the top of the mountain. I see a structure. "What's that?" I ask as I point.

"That's the Moses Memorial Byzantine Church," Laura answers.

"The what?" Jermaine asks.

"It's a church they built to honor Moses, who died on this mountain," Laura says as we continue walking. "Because the Israelites worshipped a golden calf, God forced Moses and his people to wander the wilderness for 40 years, until all the sinners had died. By that time, Moses was an old man. He'd also angered God by not doing all He commanded. So, God told Moses he couldn't enter the Promised Land. Moses led the Israelites here and before they crossed into Canaan, Moses died. At the top of Mount Nebo. As the story goes, he was one of only a few people to ever directly ascend to heaven."

"Not true," Mike says. "Sorry to interrupt you, Laura, but it's highly unlikely Moses ascended straight to heaven. Sure, his soul went there, but not this body. Human flesh cannot exist in heaven. His people buried him at the top of Mount Nebo, and they built the church over his remains."

My pulse races as we hike up a high incline. After twenty minutes of walking, we come to a large flat expanse – perfect for pitching tents.

"Let's make camp here tonight," Mike says. "I'll take you to the Ark first thing tomorrow morning."

"Thank goodness," Eli says as he puts his heavy camera equipment on the dusty ground. Eli was often ahead of us, shooting video as we climbed the mountain. He worked all the angles and recorded maybe thirty minutes of video, much of which will end up on the editing floor. He rubs his shoulders to get the blood flowing.

"We'll set up over here and start doing interviews," Marcus says. "Laura, can we start with you?"

"Sure," she says and walks over to them.

The rest of us unravel our tents and set them up in a half circle with our backs facing the base of Mount Nebo for protection. Two of Adom's crew leaves with rifles in hand. They will hunt for fresh meat. Jermaine and Adom start picking up sticks and they pile them up in the middle of camp. They then start a fire. As I take a drink of water from my canteen, I hear the crack of a rifle. The men soon return carrying a large creature with long, pointy horns. Eli gets video of them returning with their prize.

"What kind of animal is that?" I ask.

"An Arabian onyx," Adom says. "Very tasty. My men will skin it and flank it, and we'll eat like kings tonight."

My mouth waters in anticipation of the meal to come. Then my stomach starts to grumble. The greasy burger I ate for lunch does not agree with me. I grab my shovel, a roll of toilet paper, and walk over to my wife, who is sitting on a rock, rubbing her sore feet.

"Are you okay?" I ask Anna.

"Yeah, my feet hurt. How are you doing?"

"I need to use the restroom," I say as I lift the toilet paper.

"Have fun." Anna laughs. "Isn't camping great?"

"This is definitely the worst part of it. I'll be back soon."

I see bushes 100 yards ahead of our campsite and walk behind them for cover. I dig a hole, pull down my pants and squat. I hear a strange hiss. My heart stops. I glance to my right and see a large, brown-colored viper slowly slithering toward me. It locks its red beady eyes on me. I slowly stand and pull up my pants. I grab my shovel. I have no other defense. I will use the shovel to cut off its head but if I miss, it could bite me with a deadly dose of venom.

The large viper is now just a few feet from me. It lifts its head and opens its mouth. The fading sun gleams off its sharp fangs.

I slowly move the shovel in front of me to use as a shield. I am waiting for an opening to kill it, but the viper is coiled, ready to strike. It lunges at me. I block its attack with my shovel. The viper then lunges again, this time at my feet. I jump back and keep the small shovel between me and the snake.

"Agh!" I scream, afraid of being bitten.

When the snake lunges a third time, a hand appears out of thin air. Mike materializes in front of me. He is kneeling, his strong hand wrapped around the viper's neck. The snake thrashes, trying to get free, aiming its fangs at Mike's hand. Mike squeezes harder. He stands up, walks to a nearby rock, and begins bashing the viper's head against it until it's dead. He then throws its carcass off to the side.

"What was that?" I ask with fear.

"One of Lucifer's demons, trying to interfere with God's plan. Satan sent this viper to neutralize you."

"You mean, to kill me?"

"I guess you could say that. But again, that's why I'm here. To make sure you don't die."

"It took you long enough to get here," I say. "Wow, you really did a number on that snake."

Mike looks around. "You can get back to your business, Christian. It's safe."

"Thanks. Can I have some privacy?" I ask.

"You know I've been watching you go to the bathroom your entire life," Mike says.

"Gross."

"We never leave your side. I've been with you every second of your life."

"Yeah, but I've never seen you watching me go to the bathroom. Seeing you watch me is weird. It makes me uncomfortable."

Mike laughs. "Okay, I'll go back to camp. But don't take too long. I don't know what else Lucifer might try to do to stop you from uncovering God's Ark of the Covenant."

"You mean, the devil's going to come after me again?"

"You can count on it," Mike says. "But don't fear." A flaming sword suddenly appears in Mike's hand. "I'll be ready for him."

CHAPTER 13

I struggle to sleep, scared another snake will slither into my tent and poison me with its deadly venom. I know Mike watches over me, but I still struggle to trust. I struggle to truly understand the role angels play in my life. In everyone's life. Watching over us at all times? Guiding us down a certain path? It's hard to comprehend what we can't see.

Also, it's not a good feeling knowing Satan – THE Satan, king of all demons - wants me dead. What else will he do to try and kill me?

I wonder what will happen after we uncover the Ark. What does God want me to do? Does He just want me to write an article on it for National Geographic? Or will God task me with doing more?

I still can't believe God chose me, of all people. Why me? Who am I but a sinful, prideful, pitiful excuse for a human being? I'm no better than anyone else. I'm no preacher. I'm no saint. Who am I to tell others to follow God? I'm a former atheist. A hypocrite. Anna would be much better at this than me. Or Laura. But me? Seriously? God must have a sense of humor.

I hear panting outside my tent.

"Laura," I whisper. "Is that you?"

Silence. I look at Anna sleeping next to me. She doesn't stir.

I then hear a low, guttural growl outside my tent. I tense up and slowly reach for my knife, which I kept near my pillow, just in case. Whatever is out there, I am determined to protect Anna from it.

"Get!" I hear Mike yell.

I hear more growling. I quickly unzip my tent and jump outside, knife in hand. I see four wolves staring at my tent. Mike jumps in front of me.

"I said leave," Mike shouts.

The wolves attack Mike. They are biting at him with a ferocity I've never seen before. He fends them off with his hands before transforming into his angel form. Golden armor gleams off his translucent body. He rises up in the air. The bright, white light surrounding his being blinds the wolves. They flinch and whelp. A flaming sword appears in Mike's hand. He swings it violently and lops off the heads of all four wolves. Their bodies fall to the ground. Blood drains out of their necks, where their heads used to be.

Mike's flaming sword disappears. He floats back down to the ground and transforms back into his human form. I look around and see everyone is still asleep in their tents. The attack by the wolves didn't wake them.

"Come, sit with me," Mike says as he points to the fire, which still crackles.

I carefully walk around the bloody carcasses of the four massive gray wolves and follow Mike to the fire. I sit on a nearby rock and reach out my hands to warm them. I shiver. There is a chill in the night air.

"Why do you still doubt me?" Mike asks.

"I don't doubt you," I scoff.

"Come on, Chris, I know you better than anyone."

"I don't know. I mean, the things you've done. I just saw you kill a pack of wolves with a flaming sword! I feel like I'm stuck in a dream. All of this is so surreal. Honestly, though, I don't doubt you. I doubt myself."

"Why?"

"Because I'm a nobody! Why did God choose me when there are so many other people better than me?"

"Who are we to question God?" he asks. "God obviously knows best. He believes you are the perfect person to carry out this mission."

"But I don't even know the mission yet!" I say, frustrated.

"Once we uncover the Ark, I'll reveal your next steps."

"But if I knew what God wants from me ahead of time, I could prepare."

"Trust the process."

"Trust the process?" I laugh. "You make it sound like it's that easy."

"It is," Mike says. "There is so much in this world you cannot control. Why do you let fear control you?"

"Because I'm afraid of the unknown."

"Why?"

"Because it's unknown," I laugh.

"But that is when you need to lean on God. He is always here. I am always here. Guiding you. Why do you write for National Geographic?"

"Because it's fun. And I'm good at it."

"You are good at it. God gave you the talent to write. It led you toward a career in journalism. When you first applied to work for National Geographic, I made sure Jim saw your resume, and I worked with his guardian angel to encourage him to follow his gut and hire you. And he did.

"This is the path you were always meant to take. You've made choices throughout your life to follow this path. With my help and God's help, you've been able to find success as a journalist. And now, you're in a position to share the discovery of the Ark with the world. God, your guide angels, and I have put you in this position so you can become a conduit between God and humanity."

I reflect on what Mike says. I do have a broad audience as a journalist for National Geographic. People around the world will read my article. I'm in a position to write about God and His Ark and bring people closer to Him. I am now starting to see all the seeds sown during my entire life, preparing me for this moment. I better understand why God chose me. "I've always wanted my work to matter," I say.

"Writing has always been your purpose, and so far, you've done all God's intended for you. Now it's time to embrace your purpose once again."

"Which is?" I ask, hoping to finally get an answer.

"Which is soon to be discovered," Mike says cryptically. "Patience, my dear friend. Go get some sleep. Daylight will soon be here. I'll stay up and make sure Satan doesn't come after you again."

I head back to my tent, careful not to step in the blood or guts of the wolves.

"I'll clean up that mess," Mike says.

I sneak back inside my tent and hear Anna softly breathing, still asleep. I lay down next to her, close my eyes, and proceed to have nightmares of a shadow in black attacking us.

CHAPTER 14

When I open my eyes again, it's morning. Daylight shines in my tent. I lift my head and see Anna is gone. She's already awake and out of the tent.

I leave my tent and see Adom's men cleaning up the campsite. I notice the wolf carcasses are gone, as are the pools of blood caused by their beheading. Anna and Laura sit by the fire, drinking coffee. Adom and Jermaine are packing up their tents. When it comes to the wolf attack, they are none the wiser. I don't see Mike. I stroll over to the women, grab a metal cup, pick up a potholder, and grab the hot pot sitting over the fire. I pour myself a cup of coffee. I need caffeine to jolt me awake. I sit next to Anna, kiss her on the cheek, and sip my coffee.

"Big day," I say.

Anna smiles brightly. "Can't wait!"

"What do you need from me?" Laura asks us.

"Once we uncover the Ark, I'll give you time to look it over. Then we can do an interview," I say. "I'll get your impressions of it along with your Biblical expertise."

"Great," she smiles. "I am so excited about today. I just hope your friend, Mike, is right and he really does know where the Ark of the Covenant is hidden."

“Trust me,” I say. “He knows where it is. The X-ray confirmed it.”

“That’s why I’m so excited,” Laura says, “but I also know there’s a chance he’s wrong. Or maybe he made up the X-ray using AI. Or maybe we won’t be able to blast our way into the mountain.”

I point to the five boxes of dynamite. “We have enough dynamite to blow up the strongest bank safe in the world. This mountain doesn’t stand a chance.”

“I hope you’re right,” Laura says.

One of Adom’s men walks over us and puts an onyx steak on the grill next to the coffee pot. It sizzles in the fire. Fragrant smoke fills the air. My stomach rumbles with hunger.

“Are there any extra steaks? I’m starving.”

The man nods, walks away, and returns with another steak. He puts it on the grill and watches over them, so they don’t burn. I grab my plate and silverware and run water from my canteen over them. I wipe off the grease and crumbs from last night’s dinner. When the steaks are ready, Adom’s man puts one on my plate. I sit next to Anna and put the plate in my lap.

“Want some?”

“Sure!”

I cut the steak into bite-sized pieces and take turns feeding her a piece and then me. Soon, the steak is gone, and we are both satisfied.

"That was good," Anna says as she drinks from her canteen.

Mike walks into camp. "Are we ready to go?"

"Where did you go?" I ask.

"I went up ahead to scout our path to the Ark," he says.

We put our packs on our backs and follow Mike up the mountain trail. Adom's men slow us down a bit as it takes two of them to carry the boxes of dynamite. They are careful not to drop it. Eli and Marcus also slow us down as they carry their heavy gear. We are forced to navigate rocky inclines filled with brambly bushes and olive trees. After hiking for about an hour, Mike puts up his hand and we all stop.

"Is this it?" Jermaine asks as he gasps for air. We are all tired from walking.

"This is it," Mike says. He points to the side of the mountain. He then pulls out a piece of chalk from his pocket and draws a large X on the rock.

"This is it. Right here. Go ahead and blow it up," Mike says.

Adom's men get to work. They carefully set down their boxes of dynamite and take out several charges. They stack the sticks near Mike's chalked entrance and twist all the wicks into each other. They then tie on a reel of line and run it away from the blasting caps. We all follow Adom's crew around the side of Mount Nebo and kneel a good 600 feet from the blast site.

One of the men cuts the line and lights the wick. Eli videotapes all of this. We watch in wonder as the spark burns the line and flies toward the dynamite. We plug our ears. Within seconds, a large blast rocks the mountain. We feel it in our legs. Despite covering our ears, my ears ring. Dust flies around the mountain and we all begin to cough. Once we gather our wits, we follow Mike back around the side of the mountain. I am stunned to see a gaping hole where a solid sheet of rock once stood.

Mike puts his hand up.

"I only want Christian and Anna to follow me inside. For now." he says. "The rest of you, wait here."

No one protests as Anna takes her camera out of her backpack. My heart races, wondering what we'll soon see. I also grab a flashlight from my pack so we can see inside the mountain. I will light the way for Anna, so she doesn't trip over any rock fragments or other debris from the explosion.

We follow Mike into the opening in the mountain. We carefully step over rubble as I turn on my flashlight. It's hard to see as rock dust still floats in the air. I cough. We enter the darkness in front of us.

Anna falls in behind me and grabs my shirt so as not to fall. We stumble over broken rock but quickly regain our balance. We are now inside the chamber. Inside the mountain. I lift my flashlight ahead of us and see a glint of gold.

"Oh!" I yell.

"What?" Anna asks.

"I think I just saw the Ark," I say, astounded.

I shine my flashlight along the entirety of the Ark. It looks exactly like the pictures I saw on the internet. The entire Ark is covered in gold, with two golden angels on top with their wings pointing toward each other.

My flashlight starts to dim.

"Dang it," I say as I hit it on the side. "I don't have any batteries on me."

The whole room suddenly lights up. Mike has returned to his angel form. He floats. His entire being radiates a soft white light. We can now see the cavern in its entirety. It is empty save the Ark in front of us. The Ark is dusty, so I walk over and wipe off all the dust with my hands. Soon, the gold-covered box glitters from Mike's light. It's the most beautiful thing I've ever seen.

I look toward the cave entrance, afraid Adom, Jermaine, or Laura will peek inside and see Mike in his angel form, but no one is there. I blink twice in wonderment and realize there is a transparent curtain in front of the cave entrance.

"No one outside this cave can see what's happening in here," Mike explains. "Or hear what's happening in here. I put up a barrier to keep them in the dark. For now."

"Fascinating," Anna says.

"Go ahead and open the Ark," Mike says.

"Are you 100 percent sure my face won't melt?" I ask.

Mike laughs. "I promise it won't. Remember, 'Raiders of the Lost Ark' was just a movie. This is real life. God *wants* you and Anna to open it. Neither one of you will be hurt. Go ahead."

I let Anna snap her pictures of the Ark before we walk over to open it. She sets her camera on the ground and places her hands on the lid. I do the same. I half-expect to feel a jolt of electricity go through my body when I touch it, but I don't. All I feel is cold metal against my warm skin. I run my fingers under the side of the lid, looking for a grip.

And then, the most hideous wail I've ever heard suddenly pierces the air, causing us to jump back. The scream digs itself into my bones and causes my knees to buckle. Anna and I quickly cover our ears. A black shadow emerges from the darkness. It has horns growing out of its head and it breathes fire. It has a tail that snaps like a whip. As the creature emerges from the rock wall behind Anna, she grabs her camera off the ground and runs behind me for protection. I gather my strength and widen my stance, ready to fight whatever is forming in front of me. The shadow soon comes to life. A sinister face with a forked tongue and red eyes stares at me with hate. It's as if the viper I saw the day before took on a human form.

The creature leans in toward us and whispers, "How dare you enter my chamber."

"This is not your chamber, Lucifer," Mike shouts, his voice echoing within the walls of the cave. Mike rises higher and a sword of flames appears in his right hand. He swings it confidently. "It's time for you to go, Lucifer!"

Lucifer looks over at Mike and smiles. "Michael, my old friend. You don't want to hurt me. Leave me with these two. You know I have dominion over this earth. Not you."

"God still has dominion over you," Mike answers. "You cannot have Christian or Anna. God has plans for these two. But you already know this."

"Plans? What plans?" Lucifer asks.

"Enough! I'm not in the mood to play your games. You don't want to fight me. God is on my side, and you know He is more powerful than you!"

"Is He, though? Look at all the people turning away from Him. Humans are so weak. It's almost too easy to get them to follow my path over His."

"Not for long," I scream. "Once we show the world God's Ark, they will turn away from you and go to God."

Lucifer laughs at me. "You really think so? God has tried for centuries to get people to follow Him, but still, people would rather follow me than Him. I'm more fun."

"Leave now, or else!" Mike shouts.

"I'm more powerful than you in this realm," Lucifer says. A whip appears in one of Lucifer's hands while a scimitar appears in the other. He screeches. "I'm not afraid of you, Michael."

"Nor I of you," Mike says.

Lucifer swings his blade at Mike, while Mike brings his flaming sword underneath to block it. As they begin to fight, Anna and I scurry to the back of the cave, behind the Ark. We press our bodies against the rock wall to avoid getting hurt.

Lucifer cracks his whip at Mike. Mike catches the end of it and pulls Lucifer closer to him. At the same time, Mike swings his sword down on Lucifer' head. Lucifer raises his scimitar and blocks the blow. Lucifer lets go of his whip handle and drops back. Mike throws the whip to the side and grabs his sword with both hands.

"I can do this all day," Mike says with confidence.

I wonder, can Lucifer hurt Mike? Or are angels immune to injury? I don't want to find out. I want Mike to end this fight quickly.

Mike flies toward Lucifer and swings his sword. Lucifer blocks it again. He drops his scimitar and grabs Mike's wrist. Mike drops his sword, and they begin to wrestle. My mouth is open in awe. I expect Mike to win and am surprised he isn't winning easily. Mike and Lucifer roll on the ground. They punch each other. Lucifer's fingers transform into five long knives.

He pushes his hand toward Mike's shoulder, which is not protected by his breastplate. The finger-knives pierce Mike's shoulder, and he yells in pain.

Angry, Mike throws Lucifer against the wall of the cave. Mike stretches his arm, and his flaming sword flies from the ground into his hand. He steps toward Lucifer and slices at his chest. Lucifer transforms back into a shadow, and Mike's sword goes through it without causing any damage. Lucifer disappears and suddenly reappears on the other side of the chamber. It's all so fast, I can't keep track of what's happening. Everything feels surreal. Lucifer screams. Mike turns and swings his sword blindly. It slices across Lucifer's neck. The devil screams in agony and becomes a shadow once again, melting into the cave wall.

CHAPTER 15

There is silence.

"Are you okay?" I ask Mike as he floats back to the ground. He leans against the cave wall.

"Not really," Mike says as he looks at his shoulder. Gold blood stains the white tunic underneath his golden armor. "I need to go back to heaven to heal. But I can't go yet. I need to make sure Lucifer doesn't return."

"Man, Lucifer is scary," I say.

"He's not very nice," Anna says.

"No, he isn't," Mike says. "But Lucifer is right. This is his world, not mine. He has a lot more power and strength here. You see it in the number of people he's convinced to turn away from God to follow him. That's how he gains his power. When people do evil things, it strengthens him. Emboldens him. He feeds off evil deeds." Mike is breathing hard.

"I didn't know angels could get hurt," I say. "Only Lucifer has the power to hurt angels," Mike says. "We typically avoid him. No one likes him. But this confrontation was unavoidable."

"Is that your blood?" Anna asks as she points to his gold-soaked tunic.

"Yes. Angels bleed gold. But don't worry about me. It's a minor wound. God will heal me when I return to heaven."

“Does it hurt?”

Mike shakes his head. “There is no pain in heaven. I just feel… weak. But once God heals my injury, my strength will return.”

“Thanks for protecting us,” I say.

“Of course. Now, go ahead and open the Ark.”

Anna and I go back to our original positions. We both slide our fingers under the edge of the lid until we find a grip.

“On three,” I say. “One, two, three.”

We lift the lid. It’s heavy but not too heavy. It’s manageable for both of us. We slowly lower it to the ground. The white light around Mike is dimmer. He’s lost some of his energy, and it’s harder for us to see inside the cave. I ask Anna to shine her flashlight inside the Ark so we can see what’s in there. She pulls out her flashlight from her back pocket, turns it on, and aims it inside the Ark. I peer into it and see four items inside: broken shards of tablet with a foreign language engraved on them; two intact tablets with the same foreign language engraved on it; a gold jar with a lid covering the top; and a long, wooden rod with purple flowers sprouting out of it. It looks like a tree branch.

“Are those really the Ten Commandments?” I ask in astonishment, thrilled to be so close to such a coveted artifact thought to be lost to time.

"Yes," Mike says. "You're looking at the original Ten Commandments and the second pair of tablets Moses carved after he broke the first ones."

Anna takes several pictures. I open the lid to the gold jar and see white manna inside.

"Go ahead and try the bread," Mike says.

I grab the top piece of manna and take a small bite. It's fresh and tastes good.

"I thought this manna would be stale," I say.

Mike shakes his head. "Not in God's Ark."

I put the lid back on the gold jar and put it back in the Ark. I then offer Anna the piece of manna I bit into. She takes it from me and eats the rest of it.

"It's good," she says.

"Go ahead and pick up the staff," Mike says.

I reach back into the Ark and grab the staff. As I slowly lift it up, the flowers retract into the wood and disappear.

"What's going on?" I ask Mike.

"When the Israelites roamed the desert, there was conflict between the twelve tribes about which tribe would take up the priestly duties once they reached Canaan. God instructed the leaders of the twelve to leave their rods by the Ark overnight, and whichever rod produced blossoms and almonds would take on that holy role. Aaron's rod sprouted blossoms and almonds, meaning God chose his tribe to become priests. After that, whenever someone held the staff, the blossoms disappeared. Just as it did with you."

"Hmm," I mutter as I examine Aaron's rod. It's dark brown and shines in the dim light. Without flowers on it, the staff stands straight and smooth. I lower one end to the ground. It comes up to my chin.

"Aaron's staff contains some of God's powers."

"God's powers? What kind of powers?" I ask.

"When Moses and Aaron tried to convince the Egyptian pharaoh to free the Israelites, God turned Aaron's rod into a snake. When the pharaoh's magicians turned their rods into snakes, Aaron's snake ate them. Also, Aaron used his rod to spark the first two plagues in Egypt. He used it to turn all the water into blood, and he used it to summon all the frogs out of the water to infest the land. God's powers reside in this rod, and you'll be able to use some of it to legitimize your role as God's prophet."

"Can I fly? Or turn invisible?"

Mike laughs. "No, you can't fly or turn invisible, but you can teleport."

"Teleport?" Anna asks.

"Like in Star Trek?" I ask.

"Yes, like in Star Trek. Just grab the staff, announce where you want to go, and you'll magically appear there," Mike says.

"That is so cool! Does it hurt to teleport?" I ask.

"No. You blink and suddenly, you're in a different place."

"And I can go anywhere?"

"Anywhere on this planet. The staff won't teleport you to another world or to heaven. And I would avoid going to the middle of the ocean. Just for your own safety."

"Duly noted. You make it sound so easy," I say.

"It is easy. Once you get used to it. By the way, there is a caveat."

"Yes?" I ask.

"Don't let anyone else touch this rod. Just you," Mike says.

"Not even Anna?"

"Not even Anna."

"Why not?"

"God is only trusting you with His powers. No one else. If someone other than you touches this rod, they will die."

"Die? That seems a bit harsh."

"Again, this staff contains God's powers. You're lucky He's letting you borrow His powers temporarily. Humans aren't meant to have them. He's only letting you borrow them for a brief time because He knows using them will help convince others that God is real. Besides, imagine if God's powers fell into the wrong hands. It could have devastating effects on His creation.

Therefore, if anyone besides you tries to use the powers within this rod, they will die."

"Thanks for the warning," I say as I switch hands to move the rod further away from Anna.

"It's time for me to go," Mike says as he examines his wound. "When I leave, the shield guarding the entrance will disappear and your friends will be able to come inside."

"They'll ask about you," Anna says. "They'll want to know where you went."

"You can tell them the truth."

"That you're my guardian angel?" I ask.

Mike nods. "After they see what you can do with that staff, they'll have no choice but to believe you. By the way, this is the last time you will see me in human form."

"What?" Anna asks in disbelief.

"I'll still be by your side. You just won't see me. I will still communicate with you through your instinct. From here on out Christian, you'll have to make your own choices. As long as you always put God front and center, you'll be fine. Your mission now is to show the world that God exists, to show them the error of their ways, and to convert sinners into followers. I know it's a daunting task, but I will help lead you in the right direction. Just follow your gut and everything will turn out the way God intends."

I take a deep breath. "Okay. Thanks for everything, Mike. I appreciate you more than you know."

"Oh, I know," Mike says.

"That's right, you can read my mind," I laugh.

Mike winks, waves, and disappears.

CHAPTER 16

Mike is gone. I hear voices outside the cave and see Adom peek inside.

"Hello? Anyone there? Is everything okay?" Adom asks through the entrance.

"Yeah, come on in," I say.

Adom leads the way. He has a torch made from a stick, cloth, and kerosene. His fire brightens the cave.

"I've been trying to get your attention the past twenty minutes, Mr. Christian" Adom says, "but you couldn't hear me. Wait, is that the Ark?" Adom walks over and stares at it in awe. "Is it safe to touch?"

I nod. He runs his hand over the side and looks inside. "Are those the Ten Commandments?"

"Yup, the original and the second set."

The rest of our group streams in, one at a time. Eli puts his camera on his shoulder, turns on the camera light, and starts recording. Marcus holds a small boom microphone to hear us talking. Everyone's mouth drops when they see the golden Ark. They peer into it and look at both versions of the Ten Commandments along with the gold jar of manna. They begin to chat excitedly. There is electricity in the air. We've solved a 2500-year-old mystery! We've found the Ark!

Laura walks over and points at my staff. "Was that in the Ark, too? Is that Aaron's rod?"

She reaches out to grab it, and I quickly pull it away from her. "Don't touch it," I say a bit too loudly. "I'm sorry, but only I can hold this."

"Why only you?" she asks defensively. Laura looks around. "Where's Mike?"

"He left," I say.

"I didn't see him come out of the cave."

By now, everyone in the group has gathered around me and they are all staring at my rod. Anna walks in front of me and puts her hand out, urging everyone to take a step back. They comply.

"This will be hard for you understand, but I need to tell you something that will blow your mind."

"What is it?" Jermaine asks.

I take a deep breath. Will they believe me? "Mike is my guardian angel."

They all furrow their brows in confusion.

"Guardian angel? What do you mean?" Jermaine asks.

I continue. "Mike is my guardian angel. As in, he's Michael the Archangel, and he came from heaven and took on a human form for a few days to guide me. His mission from God was to lead us to this cave to recover God's Ark of the Covenant. He told me God has a special plan for me. He wants me to be His prophet and draw others closer to Him. God wants me to have the rod of Aaron because some of his powers are in it, and I'm to use those powers to get people to believe God is real."

"What you're saying doesn't even make sense," Jermaine says. "Mike wasn't human, but he was actually an angel?"

"Yes, Chris's guardian angel," Anna says. "I saw Mike in his angel form - twice. He went from human to an angel, and he had wings and was surrounded by a beautiful white light. He even fought Lucifer in this cave!"

"Lucifer, Miss Anna?" Adom asks. "We didn't hear or see anything." I can tell he still doubts.

"Mike put a veil at the entrance so you wouldn't be able to see or hear what was happening in here," I say.

Just then, we hear a high, piercing shriek. Everyone covers their ears. My heart drops. Lucifer is back! The devil once again appears from a dark shadow on the rock wall. Lucifer takes shape and towers over all of us.

"What the hell is this?" Jermaine yells as everyone scatters behind me.

"Uh, Mike, I could really use you now," I say aloud. I look around but Mike does not appear. A voice in my head say, 'You've got this. Use the rod.'

Lucifer hisses, shows us his forked tongue, and stares at me with squinty eyes. "Give me the rod."

"No!" I scream. I raise the staff and yell, "Go away! You cannot hurt us!"

A stream of golden light comes out of my staff and creates a golden dome that surrounds us, protecting us. Lucifer reaches out and touches the golden light. Sparks fly. He quickly pulls back his claw.

"Let me in!" Lucifer screams.

"No!" I yell back. "Leave. Now!" I point the staff at Lucifer and a steady stream of golden light shoots out of it. As it hits Lucifer, he screams and dissipates into smoke. He's gone. The golden shield around us disappears. All is quiet again.

"What was that?" Jermaine asks.

"Lucifer," I say.

"As in, Satan?" Jermaine asks.

I nod and extend my right arm to showcase Aaron's rod. "I told you, this staff has God's power inside it."

"Let me see," Jermaine says as he grabs the staff from me. He suddenly gasps. His face turns gray. His eyes roll in the back of his head, and he falls to the ground.

"Jermaine!" I yell.

Adom kneels next to Jermaine's body and checks for a pulse. "He's dead."

"No!" I yell. Jermaine is my best friend from college. Why did he grab the staff? Why didn't I warn him about how he would die if he touched it?

I hear a voice in my head say, 'Use the staff.'

I raise the rod over Jermaine's body and say, "Please God, bring Jermaine back to life."

Jermaine inhales loudly and opens his eyes.

"What? But... but... you were dead!" Adom says.

Jermaine sits up and looks at me. "That staff is cursed!"

"It's not cursed. It just brought you back to life," I say. "God doesn't want anyone touching it but me."

"Why you?" Jermaine asks.

I shrug. "I asked Mike that same question. All he could say is that God chose me before birth to be his prophet. I don't know why. Will you believe me now when I say Mike is my guardian angel?"

Everyone nods.

"We just saw you use Aaron's staff to protect us from Lucifer," Laura says, stunned. "I don't know what to think. All of this is so... so surreal."

"Let's focus on the Ark," I say.

Everyone walks over to the Ark. They give me a wide berth, not wanting to accidentally touch Aaron's staff.

"Is it okay to touch the Ten Commandments?" Jermaine asks.

"Yes, go ahead."

Jermaine hesitates. Laura reaches in and grabs a fragment. They both look over it in awe.

"Wow, I can't believe I'm holding a piece of the Ten Commandments," Laura says.

"I can't wait to get the Ark, the Ten Commandments, and that golden jar of manna to my lab," Jermaine says. "I'll run a bunch of tests to confirm its authenticity."

"I can arrange that right now, if you'd like," I say.

"What do you mean?" Jermaine asks.

I turn to Anna. "Are you done taking pictures of the Ark?" She nods. I turn to Eli. "Are you done filming?" He nods.

"We need more interviews. With all of you," Marcus is shaking, flustered by all he's seen. "I'd like to interview Anna first since she was the first one in the cave."

"Sure," Anna says and walks over to Marcus.

"Eli, you might want to shoot this first. Adom, can you and your men put the lid back on the Ark, please?"

They lift the lid and put it back on.

"Okay, Jermaine, grab my shirt."

Jermaine grabs a piece of my shirt. I put my free hand on the ark. "God, please take us to Jermaine's lab."

I blink and we are no longer in the cave.

Harsh luminescent lights blind my vision. I look over at Jermaine, who stands next to me with a look of shock on his face. We are now standing in his lab at his university in eastern Kansas. The Ark of the Covenant sits on the ground on my left side. Four students stop what they're doing and stare at us. One drops a beaker. It crashes on the floor and breaks the silence.

"Professor Owens?" one of the students ask.

"It worked," I say.

"Did you just teleport us from Mount Nebo to my lab?" Jermaine whispers.

"Apparently," I say, impressed with myself.

"Is that… is that the Ark of the Covenant?" a student asks.

"It is," Jermaine says proudly. "We just discovered it at Mount Nebo in Jordan, and now we're going to run tests on it to prove its authenticity." Jermaine starts shaking his arms and legs and looks over his entire body. "Wow, I can't believe you just teleported me here with that staff. Amazing! And I'm all in one piece, thank God!"

"Thank God for both of us," I say, looking up to the heavens.

"Megan, Jason" Jermaine says. "Can you put on some gloves and carefully place the Ten Commandments on this table."

Megan and Jason grab gloves, walk over to the Ark, and gently take off the lid. They begin pulling out the fragments of the Ten Commandments, gazing at them in awe.

"I need to get back to Mount Nebo," I say. "Go ahead and run your tests. I'll come back tomorrow to get your quotes for my story."

Jermaine clunkily wraps his arms around me in a hug, trying to avoid touching the staff. "Thank you. I'm so honored you took me with you on this trip." He pulls back. "I'm still processing all of this. A rod with power? The Ark? The Ten Commandments? Satan? I can't believe all this is real. My whole understanding of life is changing right before my eyes."

"That's exactly what God wants," I say with a smile. I tighten my grip on the staff and say, "God, please take me back to my wife and friends at Mount Nebo."

As the room disappears, I notice one of the students holding up a phone, recording all of it.

CHAPTER 17

I return to the cave. Everyone jumps in surprise by my sudden appearance. They ask how it went.

"It's no big deal," I say. "It doesn't hurt. You just go from here to there in a blink. Who's next?"

"Before you go again, Christian, can we interview you?" Marcus asks.

As the camera rolls, I share what happened inside the cave. I know this video will change the world for the better. Not only will they see that Lucifer is real, but they'll see how I am using God's power to beat evil.

I suddenly realize that everyone in the world will soon see this video. Soon, the entire world will know who I am. I don't feel ready for the level of fame and notoriety. I will never be able to go back to my old life, the way it was before this trip. God wants me to spread His message of love and peace and hope and good will to all, but that means Anna and I will be thrust into the spotlight. I look over at her. She seems frazzled by all she's experienced today. Everyone is shaken. And excited. And confused. Everyone is feeling a wide range of emotions as we all process the day's events.

After finishing my interview, I walk over to Anna. "How are you?" I ask.

She pushes her bangs away from her eyes. “I’m a bit overwhelmed.” I see tears start to fall down her cheeks. I extend the rod from my body, reach over, and hug her. She melts into my arms and sobs silently.

“I don’t think I’m ready for this,” she says.

“I know,” I reply. “I don’t feel ready, either. But what choice do we have?”

“I feel like all of this is being thrust upon us, like we have to do this.”

“I think we do,” I say. “I mean, God wants us to do it.”

“Just promise me we’ll do this together. That you’ll always be with me.”

I smile and squeeze her harder. “I love you so much. I’ll always be with you. I promise. As soon as Marcus finishes his interviews, I’ll take everyone where they need to go. Then we’ll go home.”

“I’d like that,” Anna says as she wipes away her tears.

After Marcus wraps up his interview with Adom, I offer to take Eli and him back to National Geographic Headquarters in Washington D.C. I grab my staff, they grab my shirt, and within a millisecond, we are no longer standing in the cave. We are now standing next to Jim’s desk. Jim is peering at his computer while drinking a cup of hot coffee. He looks over at us and jumps. Coffee spills all over his pants.

"Dammit!" he yells as he stands up. He wipes his pants, sets his cup on his desk, and looks at us incredulously. "What is going on here? Where did you come from? I thought you were in Jordan finding the Ark of the Covenant!"

"We found it," I say.

"What? Where is it?" Jim asks, looking past us.

"I took it to Jermaine's lab. He's analyzing it as we speak."

"But… but how did you get it there so quickly? Didn't you leave two days ago?"

"You're not going to believe this," Marcus says, "but we found the Ark and then Lucifer attacked us, and then Christian used his staff to protect us and then he teleported us here."

"I'm sorry, what?" Jim asks.

"I know it doesn't make much sense," I say, "but Eli has it all on video."

Eli rewinds the video in his camera and presses play. We watch on the small screen as Lucifer forms from the shadows.

"What the hell is that?" Jim asks.

"Lucifer," I answer.

"Lucifer? As in Satan?" Jim is transfixed with the video.

"Jim. I'm sorry but I can't stay. I have to get back to Mount Nebo to get my wife and everyone else home. I'll explain everything later. Just know we have great pictures and video of the Ark and the Ten Commandments. I'll start writing the story tonight and get it to you by late tomorrow. You do NOT want to sit on this, Jim. Get it out now. This is the story of our lifetime. God is making His presence known and letting the world know He is real."

Jim continues to watch Eli's video with his mouth open in shock. "This is gold, Chris. Gold!"

I grab Jim's shoulder and give him a friendly squeeze. Then I let go, grip the staff, and say, "Please, God, take me back to Mount Ebo."

I'm back inside the cave. Now it's Adom's turn. I take him and all his men (along with their supplies) back to the jeeps, so they can drive them to the airport. I then return to Anna and Laura, the only two people remaining in the empty cave.

"Honey, let's take Laura home and then we can go home."

All three of us walk outside and grab our backpacks. Laura and Anna grab my shirt, and we are suddenly no longer on Mount Nebo but standing in a home entryway. Laura gasps in delight.

"Rick? Are you here? I'm home," she says.

"Laura?" we hear a man's voice say.

"In the entryway," Laura says.

An older man with gray hair and a goatee turns the corner and smiles. "I didn't hear you come in. I thought you were going to be gone a few more days."

"Me, too," Laura says. "But we ended our trip early."

"Did you find it?"

Laura smiles. "We did."

"Really? Wow! I can't wait to hear all about it."

"Rick, this is Christian and his wife, Anna," Laura says as she introduces us. "They organized the trip."

"Thank you both for getting my wife home safely," Rick says.

"No problem." I turn to Laura. "I'll call you tomorrow to get quotes for my story."

"Of course," she says.

Not wanting to teleport in front of Rick, I open the front door, and Anna and I walk outside onto the front porch.

"Have a safe trip home," Laura says as she closes the door.

Anna grabs my shirt, and I say, "God, please take us home."

We are now standing in our living room. I sigh. We drop our backpacks on the floor, and I place the staff against the wall. To my amazement, the second I let go of it, the blossoms and almonds grow back. When I touch it, they disappear. When I let go, they grow back.

I am physically and emotionally exhausted. I'm thrilled to be back in my own home. I sit in the recliner as Anna sits on the couch.

"I'm so tired," I say.

"I don't blame you. We've had a heck of a day."

It's still light outside. I look at my watch. "It's only ten a.m. here. It feels like it should be ten p.m."

"The time difference will get you every time," Anna says.

I sigh. "I'm going to take a nap, but before I do, I want your opinion."

"My opinion on what?"

"What do you think God wants me to do with this staff?"

Anna looks at me with contemplation. "I don't know. Maybe save a life or two? Stop terrible things from happening? I don't know. What do you think?"

"I don't know. I'm confused and not sure what I should do."

"Maybe a nap will do us some good and clear our heads." Anna stands up. "Let's go."

We walk upstairs and sleep. Little did I know then, but that nap would be the last moment of peace I would ever know.

CHAPTER 18

I awake to a pounding at my front door. I wipe sleep from my eyes and look at my watch. It's 4 p.m. Anna turns to me with a worried look on her face.

"Who's that?"

I shrug.

We hear the pounding again, this time louder and harder. I get out of bed, put on my joggers, and walk downstairs. Through the glass partition, I see three men outside my door wearing black suits and sunglasses. I notice they are all wearing earpieces. Behind them sits two black sedans parked in front of our house.

"What's going on?" Anna asks as she trails me down the stairs.

"Government agents. They must know about the Ark," I say.

"How?" she asks.

"One of Jermaine's students recorded me teleporting on a phone. I'm guessing he posted it online and the video went viral."

I open the front door. "Hello?" I ask innocently.

"Christian and Anne Hagios?" the man asks. "My name is Shane Polk. I'm with the Secret Service - part of the President's advance team. The President of the United States would like to meet with you."

"Me?" I ask in shock. "Why?"

"We know you discovered the Ark of the Covenant. There's also video of you 'magically' disappearing from a lab," he says. "We're assuming it's all fake, a trick in editing to make it look like you disappeared. Or else something created by AI. But either way, we were sent here to assess the situation before you meet with the President. We've already done a background check on you and your wife. I must say, both of your credentials are impressive."

"Thank you," I say.

"Besides stealing some beer when you were in college, we couldn't find any evidence of criminal activity for either of you."

"I promise you, we are not a threat," I say. "We've been napping all day and haven't seen the video. Can you show us?"

"It's all over the internet." Shane says as he pulls out his smartphone, unlocks it, and plays the video. He presses turns his phone toward us. Anna grabs my arm as we watch. I see myself with Jermaine standing in his lab. He hugs me. I raise the staff and disappear.

"Whoa, did that dude just disappear?" a male voice behind the camera asks.

The video then shows Jermaine's students placing fragments of the Ten Commandments on a table.

"Dude, are those the actual Ten Commandments?"

"Yes, it is," I hear Jermaine say. "Steve, turn off the video. We're not ready to show this to the world yet."

The video ends. Steve obviously did not listen to Jermaine and posted it online for all to see. I look below the video box and see 130 million people have already watched it.

"It's gone viral," Shane says as he puts his phone back in his pocket. "We're here to confirm the authenticity of this video. We have agents in Lawrence right now looking into the Ark and the Ten Commandments. I'm assuming you have possession of Aaron's staff?"

"I do."

"Can I see it, please?"

"I'm sorry, but no. Only I can hold it. If anyone else touches it, they'll die."

Shane raises his eyebrow. "Are you threatening me? Liam. Kip. Secure them, please."

The other two agents tie our wrists behind our back with zip ties. We do not resist. Shane takes out his handgun and walks into our living room, looking for the staff. He finds it in the living room where I left it, leaning against the wall. He sheaths his gun and walks over to it.

"Don't touch it!" I shout.

Shane doesn't listen. He grabs the staff, convulses, and immediately falls to the ground. The staff falls to the floor next to him. His body shudders and then becomes still.

"Shane!" Kip yells. He lets go of my wrists and runs to his friend.

"Untie me," I say to Liam. "I can save him."

Liam doesn't hesitate. He takes out a knife from his front pocket and cuts the zip tie from my wrists. I run over, pick up the staff from the ground, and lean over Shane. Kip moves to the side and watches as I touch Shane's chest.

"Please, God, bring this man back to life," I say.

Shane gasps as his pulse returns.

"You're back!" Kip says loudly. Then he looks at me and says, "What the hell? Why did that stick kill Shane but not you?"

Shane coughs and breathes deeply as Kip helps him to his feet. Dazed, Shane pulls his gun and points it at me. "Drop the stick!" he shouts.

I quickly stand and say, "Turn that gun into rubber!"

Shane looks at his gun in disbelief as it transforms from metal to rubber. It sags in his hand. "What did you do?"

"Can everyone just calm down for a second. Let me explain. This is not a 'stick'." I raise the staff in the air. "This is the staff of Aaron that has been hidden inside the Ark of the Covenant the past 2500 years. God put some of His powers in this staff, and He only wants me to wield it. That is why you died after you touched it."

"I died?" Shane asks, confused.

"You weren't breathing," Kip confirms. "Christian raised the staff and asked God to bring you back to life, and that's when you started breathing again. It's as if the staff has magical powers."

Shane looks faint. He puts his rubber gun in the holster and grabs Kip's shoulder for support. "Have I been drugged? I'm confused. You're saying God put His powers in that stick? None of this makes sense."

"I know," I say. "All of this is new to me, too. But for some reason, God chose me to use the staff of Aaron and His powers to convince others to believe in Him. He wants me to be His prophet."

"God's prophet?" Shane asks.

"Man, if I hadn't just witnessed all what you just did, I would have a hard time believing all of this," Kip says.

"Okay," Shane says, in an effort to regain control of the situation, "this is all way above our pay grade. We need to take you to the President. Now."

"Can you please undo my wife, first?" I ask. Liam uses his knife to cut off her wrist ties. She quickly walks to my side.

"We have a jet waiting at the airport to take you to the White House right now," Shane says.

"We don't need a jet," I say. "Can you call the President and tell him we can meet with him right now?"

Shane looks at me with confusion. "Right now?"

"Yes, right now. Call the President and tell him that," I say.

Shane pulls out his phone and makes a call. "Hello sir, it's Shane. Are you with the President? Good. I am here with Christian Hagios and his wife. Yes, the guy who found the Ark of the Covenant. Yes, I offered to fly him to the White House to meet with the President tomorrow, but he wants to meet with him right now. Yes, right now. Yes, I know we're in Kansas City." Shane lowers his phone. "How are you going to see the President right now?"

"Go ahead and let yourselves out," I say as I grab Anna's left hand. "Are you ready to see the President?" Anna nods excitedly. I grab the staff and say, "God, please take us to the President at the White House."

Our living room disappears, and we are now standing in the Oval Office. The President of the United States looks at us from behind his desk, his mouth open in shock.

CHAPTER 19

The two agents in the Oval Office pull out their guns and level them at us.

"Freeze!" they scream.

"Turn those guns into toys," I say. Their guns turn into blue, plastic water guns. The agents look at their sidearms in disbelief. The agent closest to the President drops his toy gun and runs in front of the desk, becoming a human shield, blocking my view of the President.

I let go of Anna's hand and tighten my grip on the staff.

"Mr. President," I begin as I step to the side to see him, "please do not be alarmed. I am Christian Hagios. And this is my wife, Anna. We were told you want to talk to us?"

"What just happened?" the President asks from his chair. "How did you get in here, inside my Oval Office?"

I raise the staff. "With this, Mr. President."

"With a stick? Remind me to fire my secret service agents."

An agent off to the side lowers his phone. "I'm on the phone with one of my agents in Kansas City, Mr. President, and he says he was with Christian and his wife not five seconds ago."

"Well, how the hell did they get in here so fast, then?" the President asks.

"Like I said Mr. President, with this. The staff of Aaron."

"The what of what?" he asks.

"The staff of Aaron. I recovered – I'm sorry, we recovered it - from the Ark of the Covenant earlier today. We found it in a cave in Mount Nebo in Jordan. God put His powers in this staff, and He has commanded me to be His prophet and use it to get people closer to Him. One of the powers I am allowed to use is the power of teleportation. My wife and I teleported here from our house with this stick. I mean, staff."

"Is this some kind of elusive magic trick?" the President asks as he stands up behind his desk.

"I assure you, it is not," I say.

The agent holding the phone steps forward again. "Mr. President, my agents have confirmed the discovery of the Ark of the Covenant. And the Ten Commandments. They are both currently sitting in a lab on the campus of the University of Kansas. They also found a gold jar of manna inside the Ark. As for the staff, we don't know anything about it."

The other agent also lines up in front of me to protect the President. "I'm not going to hurt the President, I promise," I say. "And frankly, there's nothing you could do to stop me even if I wanted to hurt him."

Anna grimaces and gives me a dirty look. I can read her mind, and she's right. I shouldn't say things like that. Especially in front of the President.

"Mr. President, let me show you what I can do with this staff." I raise the staff and say, "Put the President in his pajamas."

The President's blue suit dissolves into blue satin pajamas with the Presidential seal on the left breast. The President looks down in shock. His mouth is open. I can tell he's astonished.

"What the... how?" The President is rendered speechless.

"I told you, Mr. President, God gave me this staff and these powers to do good for the world."

The President sits back down and leans back in his padded chair. He puts a finger to his chin, deep in thought. His face suddenly lights up.

"If God wants you to better this world, then you've come to the right place," the President says. "I'm the leader of the free world, and as you know, America is all about standing up for the oppressed. The weak. The poor. We show others how to properly care for the people on this planet."

I am entranced by the President. I can't believe I'm standing with Anna *inside the Oval Office!* I am face to face with the most powerful man in the world. The President is talking to me!

"What is your name again, son?" he asks.

"Christian. Christian Hagios, Mr. President." I smile, feeling star struck.

"Christian, thank you for coming to me with your newfound powers. In the wrong hands, it could be dangerous. But it looks like you're a good person. A good citizen. A good patriot."

The President pauses, so I say, "Of course, sir."

The President rubs his chin again. "I'm a good person, too. If you say God gave you these powers, then who am I to argue? I believe God put me here, in the Oval Office, to make a positive impact on the world. On America. With that in mind, I'm inclined to think God sent you to me for a reason."

Anna leans in and whispers, "I feel like he's just saying what you want to hear."

I brush her off. It's the President of the United States! Surely, he's a good person or else he wouldn't have risen so high.

"Mr. President, I will grant you one wish. Just ask and it's yours."

"I don't think that's a good idea," Anna whispers.

Concern is written all over her face. Regret washes over me. My gut tells me I might've just made a big mistake, but I let my ego overrule my gut. I want to impress the President. I decide to trust him, even as my instinct warns me to proceed with caution.

"Like a genie!" the President laughs. "One wish, eh? Together, Christian, we can do so much good in this world. I, too, want people to grow closer to God. Too many people have turned their back to Him."

"I agree," I say.

"Okay, here's my wish. The president of Russia is threatening to fire nuclear weapons at our country. To destroy America. He's already invaded the Ukraine and other nearby countries in a Russian power grab. Now he wants to destroy us. We can't allow that. Imagine what will happen if he fires nukes at our country. All of us will die. Surely God would not want that!"

I nod. "How likely is it that he'll send nukes at us?" I ask.

"It's imminent. My sources say one hundred percent. Most likely within the next few days. But you can stop him. All you have to do is kill him."

"Kill him?" I ask, stunned.

"It's him or all of America."

"But I don't think God would want me to… "

"God kills people every day. This would be one death to save millions of people, including your wife and family and friends. You would be a hero. The savior of America."

I am torn. What do I do? I imagine nuclear weapons flying toward America. It scares me. I can't let that happen. Maybe that's why God had me find the Ark and gave me Aaron's rod, to prevent a nuclear war from happening. Maybe this is my mission.

I close my eyes and ask Mike for advice. My gut tells me this is a bad idea, but then my brain contemplates life in a post-apocalyptic world. I have the power to stop it. God gave me this power. This has to be my mission, what God *wants* me to do. The President says killing the Russian president will prevent a nuclear holocaust. But I can't kill anyone. I'm not a killer. Then a loophole pops in my mind. What if I don't actually kill the Russian president but just have him touch my staff? I'll let God decide if he should die. If God wants the Russian president to live, he'll let him live even after touching Aaron's staff. If not, then he'll die. But I won't do the killing. God will. And if he dies, I will have prevented a nuclear war.

"Will I get in trouble?" I ask. "I mean, legally?"

"Nope," the President says. "I will grant you immunity afterwards. You'll be a hero. Every American will praise your name."

"So, I won't have to worry about the CIA or FBI coming to my house to arrest me?"

"Nope," the President says.

My gut still tells me this is a bad idea, but after contemplating it, I decide to do it. I mean, the President of the United States wants me to do it. He says there's an impending nuclear war if I don't. He would know. What choice do I have? If I can't trust him and his judgment, who can I trust?

"Okay," I say. "I'll do it."

The President smiles. I look at Anna, who looks terrified. "Are you sure you want to do this?" she asks.

"I truly think this is why God gave me His powers," I say. "To prevent a nuclear war. You heard Mike. He said God wants me to save the world. I think this is how God wants me to do it."

"Okay," she says hesitantly.

I raise the staff and say, "Take me to the Russian president."

The Oval Office disappears. I am now standing outside with colorful Russian buildings in the shapes of flower bulbs all around me. There is a chill in the air. I can see my breath, and I shiver. I should've worn a coat. I look around and see a large group of important-looking Russians gathered in front of me. They are all shocked by my sudden appearance. A dozen soldiers standing nearby quickly raise their rifles at me.

"Turn those guns into bananas," I say. All their rifles suddenly turn into bananas. The soldiers look at the bananas with confusion, unsure what to do next.

An older man steps forward and yells at me in Russian. I don't know what he is saying. Is this the President? "Help me understand Russian." I say as I raise the staff.

I suddenly understand every word he is saying.

"How dare you interrupt us, you insolent jerk! Who are you, anyways, and where did you come from? Do you know who I am?"

"You're the president?" I ask in Russian.

"That's right! I am the ruler of Russia. How dare you interrupt our ceremony!"

"Here!" I say, and I lob the staff toward him. In midair, flower blossoms and almonds appear on the staff. When the Russian president catches it, the blossoms and almonds disappear. He then falls to the ground, lifeless. The staff clatters on the hard pavement and the blossoms and almonds reappear. I step toward his body, pick up the staff, and say, "Take me back to the Oval Office." I reappear in front of the President and Anna.

"It's done," I say.

A red phone on the President's desk suddenly rings. He picks it up and listens to the voice on the other end. After a few seconds, he hangs up.

"Boris Slentsky is dead. However, journalists caught you on camera throwing him your staff right before he died. It will soon be all over the news. I need one more favor, Christian."

"Yes, Mr. President."

"It cannot be known that I authorized this. Russia would still attack us with nuclear weapons if they discovered I had anything to do with this. I need you to take sole credit. Do you understand?"

"Yes, Mr. President," I answer.

"This magical stick you have is pretty amazing. The entire world will soon know about it thanks to this video. As long as you continue to say God gave it to you, that God sent you to kill him to save our country from a nuclear attack, then everything will be okay."

I feel bad blaming God. Is that the right thing to do? Will God be mad at me?

I hear a voice in my head say, 'What have you done?'

I immediately feel regret. Should I go back and bring the Russian president back to life?

'It's too late,' the voice in my head says. I know it's Mike.

What have I done? I thought it was the right move! 'Why didn't you stop me?' I yell in my brain to Mike.

'I wanted you to make your own choice,' I hear Mike say. 'Free will.'

'But I screwed it all up!' I yell again in my head.

'Maybe. We'll see. You'll just have to live with the consequences.'

'Is God mad at me?" I ask.

'Of course not. He's disappointed, but He has faith you will make amends. This is what free will looks like, Chris. Sometimes you make good choices. Sometimes you make mistakes. But the true test of a soul's character is what do you do after you make a bad choice.'

'But I thought I could trust the President!'

'Now you know you can't,' I hear Mike say.

I look at the President. "Mr. President, I need to get back home." I want to get to a safe space with Anna and regroup to figure out my next move.

"Thank you, Christian. You've done your country a great service today."

I frown, grab Anna's hand, and take us back home, wondering how I'm going to handle the fallout from my mistake.

CHAPTER 20

It grows dark outside. I lean the rod against the wall, sit on the couch, and exhale. I feel the stress of the day melt away as I settle into the comfy cushions. Anna sits next to me but doesn't say a word. I know she has something to say. After twenty years of marriage, we have a rhythm. I instinctively know what she's going to say before she opens her mouth. I also know she won't be denied her opinion. She's going to tell me her thoughts whether I like it or not.

"I think you made a huge mistake," she says.

I hang my head. "I know. I'm sorry. I thought I was doing the right thing. I mean, the President of the United States said this was the only way to stop a nuclear war."

"He was very convincing," Anna says, "but he also asked you to kill someone. God is all about love, not murder."

"Technically, I didn't kill him," I say. "God did. I simply gave him Aaron's staff."

Anna shakes her head. "You threw it at him. A person's instinct when something is thrown at them is to catch it. You knew what you were doing. And you knew what would happen if he touched the staff. You allowed it to happen."

I hang my head even lower. I know she's right. "I'm sorry. I must be such a disappointment."

Anna puts her arm over my shoulder and hugs me. “Hey, I love you. We’ll get through this. I just think you need to refocus and only do good things from here on out. Help people, don’t hurt them. No more death.”

“I agree,” I say as I look into her beautiful brown eyes. “Mike chastised me afterwards.”

“He did?”

“Yeah, in my head. I could hear his voice. He said it was okay I made this one mistake but now I need to live with the consequences.”

“Which are?”

“I don’t know. I guess we’ll find out. I hope it doesn’t involve prison time.”

“The President said he would pardon you if it came to that.”

“Yeah, but can I trust him?”

Anna shrugs and pulls her cellphone out of her pocket. I realize I left my phone upstairs and never grabbed it after my nap. Oh, well. I hardly use it, anyways. I grab the remote control and turn on the television as Anna answers her phone.

“It’s my mom,” she whispers.

I turn it to a news channel on the TV as Anna begins talking to her mom.

"Hi mom. Yes, I know it's unbelievable. Yes, I promise, it's all real. Yes, Chris and I uncovered the Ark of the Covenant." Anna looks at me. "I'll be right back." She stands and walks into the kitchen.

I turn my attention to the TV. A news program called "The Breaking Point" is playing the video of me disappearing from Jermaine's lab. Then they play video of the Russian President grabbing my staff and falling to the ground, dead. You see me quickly pick up the staff and disappear.

An anchor comes on and begins talking.

"You are watching 'The Breaking Point'," she says. "I'm your host, Amy Morgan. Tonight, we will discuss the strange death of Russian President Boris Slentsky, just seconds after a stranger appeared near him while holding a long walking stick. Slentsky touched the stick and suddenly died. It appears this man is the same one who appeared to magically disappear from a lab in Kansas, where the Ark of the Covenant is allegedly being held.

"Sources have helped us identify the disappearing man as Christian Hagios of Kansas City. Our sources also tell us Hagios and a group of archeologists found the Ark inside a cave in Mount Nebo in Jordan earlier today. The Bible notes the staff of Aaron was left inside the Ark. Might this be the stick Hagios is holding? And does it truly have powers? Or is this all of this just one big, elaborate hoax?

"To answer those questions, we turn to Pat McMurtry, the U.S ambassador to Russia. Pat, what is the President saying about the death of Russian president Slentsky?"

The camera shot goes to Pat McMurtry, who is live via satellite from Moscow. He clears his throat and says, "The President tells me he had no previous knowledge that Christian Hagios was going to use an ancient artifact to kill the Russian president. His sudden appearance, judged by many experts, appears to be some kind of magic trick. A hoax. Jordan is not far from Russia, so he could've easily traveled to Moscow after finding the Ark with the intent to kill Slentsky. As for the video from Kansas, that could've easily been created using AI."

Pat continues. "Many think Hagios is justifying his actions by claiming God gave him special powers and ordered him to kill Slentsky. I spoke with an epidemiologist who believes there might be an ancient virus on the stick. He believes that is what caused the Russian president to die so suddenly."

"But if that's the case, why hasn't the virus killed Christian Hagios?"

"Some people are naturally immune to certain diseases. My guess is he's immune to this ancient virus. Let me repeat myself: The President told me he does not know Christian Hagios, and he says Hagios did this without any authorization from the United States."

"Wow," Amy says. "By the way, we have not heard from Hagios, so we don't know his motivation. However, as we've reported here in recent days, Slentsky had been threatening the United States with a nuclear attack. Pat, do you think his death might've saved American lives?"

Pat sighs. "Potentially. Yes, Slentsky was threatening to fire nuclear warheads at us, but there is no confirmation an attack was imminent."

"That very well could've been Christian's motivation. To speak more on this, we are joined on the phone with one of Christian's friends." Amy cups her ear to hear her producer talking in her earpiece. "His name is Jermaine Smith and he's an anthropology professor at the University of Kansas. He is currently in possession of the Ark of the Covenant and is testing its authenticity. He is also in possession of both sets of the original Ten Commandments, and a gold jar of manna, as was said to be inside the Ark. My first question for you Jermaine: Is this Ark legit? Is this the Ark from the Bible?"

"It is," Jermaine says over the phone.

"Honey, you should come out here and watch this," I shout to Anna.

"I'll talk to you later, mom," Anna says as she comes back from the kitchen. She hangs up and sits next to me.

"What did you find inside the Ark?" Amy asks Jermaine.

"We found Aaron's staff, a gold jar filled with manna, and the broken pieces from the first set of Ten Commandments, along with the second complete set of the Ten Commandments."

"Amazing! You told us you were with Christian Hagios when you found the Ark. Do you really believe there are powers in Aaron's staff?"

"I do. I've seen Christian use these powers."

"How?" Amy asks.

"He battled Satan with that staff."

"Come on!" Pat says. "Satan? Do you think this is a joke? Your friend killed Russia's president with this stick and now our county is facing a major crisis as Russia threatens to attack us."

"Christian told me the powers in the staff come from God."

"God? Do you really think God encouraged Christian to kill Russia's president?" Pat asks. "God is all about love, not murder."

"Is he though?" Jermaine asks. "Have you read the Old Testament? God kills a lot of people in that part of the Bible. Take Noah's Ark. God drowned the whole world. Now I will say, I've only read the Bible as a scholar as I am an atheist. Or should I say *was* an atheist until I saw what Christian did with that staff. He teleported me from Jordan to my lab in Kansas. I can't deny it. That staff truly does have powers within it."

"Still, you truly think God put His powers in a stick and told Christian to go kill Russia's leader?" Pat asks. "Please!"

"I'm not saying God told Christian to kill Russia's president, and I know it's hard to believe, but there is no other explanation other than to say the powers of that staff come from God. God chose Christian to find the Ark. God wants Christian to use the staff to bring us closer to God.

"As for killing Russia's president, I think that was a mistake. I've known Christian for 20 years and he won't even kill a spider. He'd rather take it outside and let it go.

"I'm telling you, as a person who's never believed in God, after what I've seen, I believe in God now."

"What else can Christian do with that staff?" Amy asks.

"As I said, he can teleport..."

"That's not even scientifically possible," Pat shouts, frustrated. "Now this guy is just making stuff up."

"Yes, teleportation has not been proven by science," Jermaine continues, "but neither has the existence of God. And I'm telling you, after all I've seen these past 24 hours, I can now say without a doubt that God exists."

"You should get this guy off the show," Pat tells Amy. "He's just feeding you lies. God? Powers? Come on. It's not real. He's making all of this up to justify his friend's actions."

I feel my face flush as I become angry. How dare they doubt God! Jermaine just told them the truth and they don't believe him? What more proof do they need?

An idea pops in my head. I stand up and grab the staff.

"Where are you going?" Anna asks with an air of concern.

"I'll be right back," I smile at her, confident this will work. "Take me to the "Breaking Point" studio."

I am suddenly standing next to Amy, whom I just saw on my television screen a second ago. She stops talking midsentence and looks at me with her mouth open, surprised. I see some other people in the studio. Two are behind large studio cameras. A producer stands nearby with a headset on. I look up and the studio lights blind me. I turn to Amy.

"Hi," I say. "I'm Christian Hagios. You were just talking about me?"

"Uh, yes. Yes, we were," she says. Amy points to an empty chair on her left. "Would you like to have a seat? Mark, can you get a mic on Mr. Hagios?"

I sit in an empty seat to her left as the producer with the headset runs up to me and clips on a small microphone to my shirt. He sets a power box in my lap and goes back to where he was standing. The cord dangles in front of my shirt.

"How did you do that? Appear in our studio like that?" she asks.

“My friend, Jermaine, was telling the truth,” I say. “God granted me the use of some of His powers, which are embedded inside this staff of Aaron.” I have the staff in my left hand, and I raise it for show. “We found this earlier today in a cave in Mount Nebo in Jordan inside the Ark of the Covenant. I’m just getting used to the powers God granted me.”

“So, you honestly believe God gave you special powers. Why you?” she asks.

I look straight into the camera. “God is frustrated with how many people no longer believe in Him, so he assigned me the task of convincing you He is real. God wants me to be His prophet. He wants me to remind you how wonderful He is. If you would just believe, then you will be guaranteed entrance into heaven when you die…”

“Okay, okay, enough about God and heaven,” Jim says. I can hear his voice over a speaker in the studio “I want to know who gave you the authority to kill Russia’s president?”

“That was a mistake,” I say. “I’m sorry about that. I wish I could take it back. But I was told the Russian president was about to fire nukes at America, and I felt I had to do something. I promise you, I am not a killer. In retrospect, I wish I would’ve done something else to stop the nuclear attack.”

“Like what?” the female anchor asks.

“Like turn all the nuclear warheads into paper airplanes.”

An idea pops into my head and I raise my staff. "God, please turn every nuclear warhead in the world into a paper airplane." I pause a second and then say, "Done."

"How do you know?" Amy asks me.

"I just do. I'm sure you'll soon learn soon enough that there are no more nuclear warheads in this world."

"Why are you making up lies like this?" Pat asks. "We're facing an international crisis because of you!"

"That's why I'm here," I say, "to apologize and let the entire world know that from now on, I plan to use God's powers for good. I promise."

"God's powers?" Pat scoffs. "More like magic tricks."

"I am not performing magic tricks." I tighten the grip on my staff. "I don't know magic. Only the power of God. To prove it to you once again, watch this." I take off my microphone, set it on the anchor desk, and stand up. "God, please take me back home."

I am suddenly back home, sitting on the couch, watching the TV. Amy reacts to my sudden disappearance.

"Whoa, where did he go?" she asks. "If that's a magic trick, it's really good one. I… I don't know what to think. Pat, do you think Christian's apology is enough?"

"He seemed sincere, but he still killed Boris Slentsky. I highly doubt Russia will accept his apology."

"At least it's a start," Amy says.

"Wow, that was really cool how you did that," Anna says. "To see you standing here and then suddenly you were inside the TV – wow!"

"What do you think? Did I do the right thing?" I ask.

"Going on that show will certainly help improve your image," Anna says.

"I felt like I needed to do something big to change people's minds about me," I say. "I feel like most people think I'm evil."

"I wouldn't say evil. Maybe misguided. Some might even appreciate the fact you prevented a nuclear war. I like how you said you made a mistake and apologized. It makes you human. You're showing the world that even a human with God's powers can make a mistake."

"I hope they see it that way," I say. "I mean, I truly don't know what I'm doing. I never wanted these powers. I'm doing the best I can."

Anna puts her arm around me. "I think we should eat dinner and go to bed. It's been a long day. We can regroup in the morning. I have an idea for you."

"What's that?"

"What if tomorrow, you went to Children's Mercy Hospital and healed a bunch of sick kids?"

"I like it. Should I call ahead or just show up?"

Anna shrugs. "Either way, it's a wonderful way to repair your image and use God's powers for good. Hopefully doing something like that will change people's opinion about you."

CHAPTER 21

The sun pierces through our bedroom blinds, warming my eyes and waking me from my slumber. I wipe the sleep from my eyes, stretch, and grab my phone off the charger. I intentionally have not looked at it since leaving Jordan. I knew I'd be bombarded with calls, texts and emails, and I just didn't want to deal with it. But now I figure I should see who's been trying to reach me.

I have 56 text messages, 109 emails and 14 missed calls. I look at the calls first. I see Jermaine called five times. Jim, my boss at National Geographic, also called multiple times. As did my mom. I turn toward Anna and gently rub her shoulders.

"Time to wake up," I say.

"But I'm so tired!" she groans.

"It's eight o'clock."

She opens her eyes and smiles. "Today's a big day!"

"I have a feeling every day from here on out is going to be a big day for us," I say. "Life will never be the same."

"I think you're right. It's God's will for us. Who are we to argue?"

"I already lost that argument with Mike. Might as well embrace our purpose. Before I go to the hospital, I'm going to make some calls. I have a lot of catching up to do."

She kisses me, gets up, and goes to the bathroom. I pull my pillow up against the headboard and push myself up. I call Jermaine first.

"Chris! Where have you been? I called you ten times last night."

"Sorry, I've been away from my phone. I heard you on that news program last night."

"I know. I saw you appear on air. How crazy was that!"

"I didn't like how they refused to believe you, so I thought I would go there and convince them otherwise. I am a prophet of God."

"I know that now," Jermaine says. "Chris, I have everyone calling about the Ark. All the major news outlets, TV and print. They all want to come here to get video, pictures, and interviews. What's your deal with National Geographic? Is the Ark exclusive only to them?"

"It is," I say. "Don't let anyone in to see it. I'll ask Jim about your request after I get off the phone with you and email you his response. I can't believe one of your grad students leaked video of me leaving your lab."

"If anything, it's brought more attention to this story. Now everyone wants to know more about the Ark. I've had a line of colleagues coming in and out since last night, wanting to see the Ark for themselves. I've been letting them take pictures with it."

"Jermaine! Please don't let anyone else photograph it. For now."

"Okay, boss."

"Have you done any testing on it?"

"I've been here all night doing various tests. I can confirm the Ark is around 2500 years old."

"Was there any doubt?"

"Not really, but at least my tests will verify our story. You should consider having a third-party test it as well for verification."

"I'll see what Jim wants to do. Can you email me your reports? I'll need them for my story. I'm supposed to write it today."

"Sure! I'll send them over right away."

"Thanks, Jermaine. I'll talk to you soon."

I hang up and call my boss.

"You're a hard man to reach," he says. "I've seen all sorts of videos and pictures online. I thought we had a deal, and *we* had exclusive rights to the Ark."

"You still do. I'm sorry. I can't control Jermaine's students or his colleagues."

"You're fine. But I do want to fast track this story and get it to print as soon as possible. I'd also love for you to include your experiences with the staff of Aaron. Eli is nearly done editing. We're going to broadcast your journey to finding the Ark tonight. A special report."

"You're certainly striking while the iron is hot."

"We have to. I feel like we've already lost control of this story. It truly is the greatest story of our time. You find the Ark and a staff with powers embedded in it? This whole thing is so surreal."

"Tell me about it," I say. "A ton of media wants to see the Ark and do a story on it. What should I tell Jermaine?"

"Tell him after our special airs tonight, he can talk to the media and let them see the Ark. But not until tomorrow."

"Got it. I'll tell him."

"Also, just so you know, the video Eli shot of Satan? It's all digitized. None of it is usable."

"But we watched it in your office."

"Something happened to the video when Eli downloaded it into the editor," Jim says. "It's no longer usable."

"Shoot. Okay."

"Can you please have Anna send over her pictures as soon as possible? And can you get me your article by noon your time?"

"Will do," I say. "We'll talk soon."

I hang up and call Laura. "Laura, it's Christian."

"My God, Christian, what have you done? God grants you power, and you use it to kill Russia's president?"

My heart drops. I hate disappointing people. "I made a mistake and won't do it again. Trust me. Anyways, the reason I'm calling is that my publisher wants my story by noon. Could you write your thoughts on the Ark and send it over to me as soon as possible, please?"

"I already wrote out my thoughts. I have your email and will send it to you right away."

"Thanks!" I hang up and yell at Anna in the bathroom.

"Did you hear all that?"

"Got it. I'll get those pictures over by noon."

I look on my phone and click on the news apps to see what they're saying about me. The top story headline reads "Mystery Man Kills Russian President".

I read the article.

"Moscow, Russia --- Russian president Demetri Slentsky is dead, and the search is on for the mysterious man believed to be responsible. Russia media caught the mystery man on camera. Sources have identified him as Christian Hagios of Kansas City. He was holding a walking stick, presumably the staff of Aaron, which sources say he discovered earlier in the day when he uncovered the Ark of the Covenant, as described in the Bible. A group of explorers, including Hagios, claim to have found the missing artifact inside a cave at Mount Nebo, Jordan. According to legend, the staff has magical powers. Witnesses claim the alleged assassin appeared out of thin air, though some experts are calling his sudden appearance in Moscow a highly sophisticated hoax. Experts also believe an ancient virus on the staff might be responsible for the Russian president's sudden death."

I raise my hands in disbelief. They're calling me an alleged assassin? Oh boy. How do I escape that label?

I continue to read. "Video also shows Hagios vanishing from a lab at the University of Kansas, where the Ark is currently being held as experts verify its legitimacy. Witnesses say when Hagios appeared in Moscow, he 'used magic' to turn Russian soldiers' guns into bananas. When President Slentsky touched the staff, he immediately fell to the ground, dead. Hagios then grabbed the staff and once again vanished. Russian officials say they want justice against the man responsible.

"This man who killed our President must be punished," said Vladmir Solotsky, Russia's interim president. "I call for all Russians to find him and bring him to us so he can be prosecuted for what he's done."

"This incident is causing our relationship with Russia to be more strained than ever," said Brenden Burks, an advisor to the

President. "The President would like to talk to this Christian Hagios and help Russia bring him to justice."

But the President promised me immunity. I feel sick. Has he changed his mind? Am I truly a wanted man? I continue reading.

"Hagios appeared on the TV show, "The Breaking Point" last night. He claimed God put powers in the staff of Aaron and chose Hagios to be his prophet. Efforts to reach Hagios for comment have so far been unsuccessful."

I scan a couple other articles. They all say the same thing, accusing me of being an assassin. Tired of reading about my mistake, I jump out of bed, take a shower, and put on some fresh clothes. After eating a bowl of cereal and calling my mom back, I sit down at my computer and print off Jermaine's lab reports and Laura's testimony. I spend the next few hours putting together the first draft of my article for National Geographic. Anna is in the basement developing her film. I look at my watch. It's eleven o'clock. We'll have to send it all over to Jim within the hour.

The doorbell rings. I walk over and open the front door. A female reporter with a microphone stands on my stoop. A man with a video camera on his shoulder stands behind her. I see a red light up top. He's rolling.

"Christian Hagios? I'm Kathy Bergstrom from the local Fox affiliate. Can I ask you a few questions?" She hands me her business card, and I slip it in my jeans pocket.

"Sure," I say as friendly as possible. I knew news reporters would eventually descend upon my house. That's why, while eating breakfast, I plotted what I would say to their questions.

"Did you kill the president of Russia?"

"No, my staff did," I say. I look past Kathy and see half a dozen news vehicles parked on the street. Reporters and photographers are now running toward me. I pause and wait for all of them to approach so I don't have to repeat myself.

"Hold on," I say. I walk upstairs and grab Aaron's staff. I know they'll want to shoot video of it.

I step back out on the stoop and start talking as reporters jam microphones and tape recorders near my mouth. "Yesterday morning, I took a team of people to Mount Nebo in Jordan to find the Ark of the Covenant. We used a high-tech radar and found it hidden inside a hidden cave. As we recovered the Ark, an angel came to me and told me God wanted me to be his prophet. God put some of His powers into the staff of Aaron, which I am holding right here, and the angel told me to let the entire world know that God is real, and that He loves all of His creation.

"To prove God is real, He's allowing me to use some of His powers. This is not a magic trick. I don't know magic. These powers I have are from God. Watch." I raise the staff. "God, please take me to Smith Park."

Smith Park sits three blocks from my house, and I suddenly appear there. I count to ten and say, "God, please take me back to my front stoop." I am back in front of the reporters. They all gasp.

"How did you do that?" Kathy asks.

"I told you, God gave me the power to do it. That's how I got home from Mount Nebo. And from Russia."

"Why did you kill Russia's president?" another reporter asks.

"I made a mistake. I didn't know he would die if he touched the staff." I lie. I've decided that stretching the truth will be the best way to get the world to forgive me. Heck, my guardian angel used lies to hide the truth. Why not me? Only Anna, the others who went with me to Mount Nebo, and the Secret Service agents who visited me last night know that if someone touches the staff, they will die.

"But in the video, you threw him the staff. As if you wanted him to hold it. If God put powers in it only for you, why would you freely give it to him?"

Great question. I didn't have an answer. I hadn't thought ahead on how to answer that one.

“Ugh,” I stammer. “It slipped out of my hand as I walked toward him.”

“Do you think an ancient virus on your staff killed him?”

“Maybe,” I say. “It makes sense.” I don’t want to blame God. I want people to believe in a loving God, not fear a God who might hurt them.”

All the reporters step back, not wanting to stand too close to the staff I’m holding.

“I have been tasked with spreading God’s love to everyone in the world. I feel horrible that someone died from this staff. I’ll be more careful from now on. I want to use God’s power for good and improve peoples’ lives.”

“How?” Kathy asks.

“By healing the sick and showing the world that God is real. God exists. I doubted the existence of God for a long time. But how can I doubt Him now? The powers He’s given me is proof enough. You just saw me use them.

“I plan on going to Children’s Mercy this afternoon to heal some sick kids. Let’s say one o’clock. Meet me there with your cameras and I will show you all the good I can do with the staff of Aaron. That’s all I have for now. Thanks for stopping by.”

I step back into my house and close the door. Anna stands behind me.

“Who was that?”

"Local reporters," I say. "Are your pictures developed?"

"They are. I already sent them over to Jim."

"How did they come out?"

"Great! Unfortunately, I didn't get any pictures of Mike or Lucifer. Just the Ark and our discovery of it."

"I'm pretty sure neither Mike nor Lucifer want their picture in National Geographic," I joke. "In fact, Jim told me the video Eli shot of Lucifer was all digitized, so they didn't get him on camera either. I'm pretty sure Lucifer wants to stay in the shadows when it comes to publicity."

"Good point. Are you done with your writing?"

"Just about." I walk to my desk and lean my staff against the wall. I sit down, wake up my computer, and re-read my article. I make some changes as Anna goes into the kitchen to make lunch. At 11:59, satisfied with my writing, I send it over to Jim. I know he'll have his own edits.

Someone rings the doorbell.

"I'll get it," I yell to Anna in the kitchen. "It's probably another reporter."

I grab the staff and head to the front door. I open it, and see a short, older white man standing alone. He wears a brown trench coat and a brown hat over his gray hair. He looks like he stepped out of an old episode of 'Columbo'.

"I told the other reporters to meet me at Children's Mercy at one o'clock..."

"I'm not a reporter," the man says with a gravelly voice. "Christian? My name Is Roger Officer."

"You're a police officer?"

"No. My last name is Officer. I'm CIA."

Roger pulls out an ID and flips it toward me. I read the letters C.I.A. It looks official.

"CIA? Why are you here?"

Roger laughs. "You shouldn't be surprised. You've created an international crisis by killing Russia's president. May I come in."

I grip the staff. "Are you going to hurt us?"

Roger laughs again. "No, I'm here by order of the President of the United States to protect you."

I let Roger in and lead him to the kitchen. Anna is in the process of making sandwiches.

"Hungry?" I ask.

"No, thanks," Roger says.

"Anna, this is Roger Officer. He's a CIA agent."

"From the Kansas City office. Mind if I sit?"

Roger sits at the table and pulls out a brown envelope from the inside pocket of his trench coat. He opens it up and pours the contents on the table. I see two credit cards and two

Missouri driver's licenses with our pictures on them. The names on the licenses read Darryl and Lilly Young.

"What are those?" I ask.

"Fake IDs. For you and your wife. And new credit cards, so no one can trace them and find you."

I lean my staff against the wall, and Anna and I sit down at the table.

"What's going on?" Anna asks.

"You and your husband are in danger," Roger says. "The President has asked us to protect you, as secret agents from Russia and other parts of the world want to either kill you or take you into custody."

"Kill me?" I ask with concern.

"Yes, some want you dead, Mr. Hagios. Frankly, I'm surprised the President didn't ask us to take you into custody considering you killed the president of Russia, but he gave us strict orders to protect you and let you continue doing what you're doing. You must have some pretty powerful friends high up on the food chain."

I look up toward the heavens and smile. "I do." I look back at Roger and ask, "What are the fake IDs for?"

"I want you and your wife to leave your house as soon as you can. Check into a hotel and use a fake ID and credit card to get a room. Stay hidden, so no one can find you."

"For how long?" Anna asks.

"I'm not sure," Roger says. "I'll have an agent watch over your house. When all this blows over and things are safe again, I'll give you the all clear to return home." Roger reaches into his pocket and pulls out a phone. "This is how we'll communicate. Leave your phones here. That way no one can trace them and find you. Call me once a day on this phone, and I'll let you know when it's safe for you to come back. Okay?"

Anna grabs my hand. "I don't like this, being in danger."

"I'm sorry, ma'am, but it'll blow over. Trust me. It always does."

"Anything else we need to know?"

"You said you're going to Children' Mercy today? I'll send an agent over to watch the outside of the hospital to make sure you stay safe."

"Thank you," I say as I stand, cuing Roger to leave. Roger stands up, and I walk him to the door.

"Thanks for looking out for us," I say as I shake his hand.

Roger looks me in the eye. "This is not my idea. If it were up to me, you'd be behind bars right now. But I have my orders. You have my word that my agents will do everything in their power to protect you from any threats. But like I said earlier, go to a hotel and hide out for a few days, just in case."

I bid him farewell and rejoin Anna in the kitchen.

“Should we stay hidden?” Anna asks.

“God wants me to perform miracles right now, so I’m going to say no,” I answer. “I need to be out there in public, showing people God’s powers.”

“Should I be worried about our safety?” Anna asks.

“No,” I say with confidence. “God’s got this. He’ll protect us. At least my staff will.” I nod at the flowering staff leaning against the wall. “I do think we should go to a hotel when I get back from Children’s Mercy.”

“I can pack while you’re gone,” Anna says.

“Perfect,” I say as I sit down and eat the sandwich Anna made me. As we eat, we talk about God’s will for us, and how we’ll handle all the changes in our lives.

“I really need your support in all of this. I need you by my side,” I say to Anna.

She reaches over and grabs my hand. “I’m not going anywhere.”

“A part of me wishes you were the one chosen by God, not me. You’d be so much better at all of this,” I say.

“Not necessarily,” Anna says. “I believe God chose you for a reason. Maybe He chose you because you doubted His existence for most your life. You’re a walking, living, breathing testimony into how someone can change their beliefs once they know God is real”.

"You're right, as usual," I say. "I love you so much. I just hope this mission of mine brings us closer together. It's been a rough few weeks."

"Yes, it has," Anna says with a sad smile. "But knowing our son is in a better place has helped me handle his loss in our life much better than before."

"Me, too," I say as I reach over and squeeze her hand. I look at my watch and see it's almost one o'clock. "Oh, I've got to go."

"Where?"

"To Children's Mercy Hospital. It was your idea. I told all the reporters to meet me there at one, so they can see me heal the sick."

"I love it. You're going to make a huge difference."

"I certainly hope so. See you later!"

I stand up, grab my staff, and say, "Take me to Children's Mercy Hospital."

CHAPTER 22

I stand in the lobby of Children's Mercy Hospital. Everyone near me stares in disbelief, stunned by my sudden appearance. They point, whisper, and step back. The same reporters who were on my front porch earlier in the day walk up to me. They've been waiting. Taking the lead, I casually walk up to the guard at a nearby desk. He's the gatekeeper into the hospital. He missed my sudden appearance as he was looking down at his phone when I arrived. He looks up at me with a frown. He does not recognize me.

"I need an ID," he says. "Who are you here to see?"

"I'm Christian Hagios, and I'm here to heal some of the sick kids in your hospital," I say, hoping my name rings a bell with him. Nothing.

The guard raises an eyebrow. "Are you a doctor?"

"No, a prophet of God," I say. I pull my real ID from my wallet and give it to him. The camera operators press record to catch the moment on tape.

He looks down and writes my name on a logbook. "A prophet? You need to leave." He hands me my ID and points to my staff. "Besides, there are no weapons allowed inside the hospital."

"This isn't a weapon," I say as I raise my staff. "This is the staff of Aaron, filled with the powers of God to heal all the children here."

The guard looks at me as if I'm crazy. He presses down on the walkie talkie attached to his chest and calls for backup.

"Are you going to leave quietly or do I need to force you to leave?" he asks me.

"Eddie, don't you recognize this guy?" asks another guard who walks up behind Eddie.

"No. Who is he?"

"He's all over the internet. He says God gave him powers in that staff."

"Should I let him in?"

"Call media relations. Let them deal with him."

Kathy Bergstrom, steps forward. "I called ahead to media relations. Abby is supposed to meet us here," she tells the guards.

"Here I am," says Abby as she rounds the corner and walks over toward us.

I step aside as a father pushes his daughter in a wheelchair toward the guard.

"We have an appointment," the father says.

"What's wrong with your daughter?" I ask.

He turns to me and says, "Spina bifida. She can't walk."

"May I?" I ask.

Her father gives me a cautious look, wondering what I'm going to do, but he allows me to put my hand on his daughter's head. I close my eyes, grip my staff, and say, "Dear God, please use your powers to heal this young girl. Amen."

I open my eyes and remove my hand. The young girl squeals in delight. She starts moving her legs and her toes. The people around us gasp in disbelief. The camera operators step in closer to get shots of this miracle. The young girl stands and starts walking.

"Dad, look! I can walk!"

I see her dad weeping. "How did you do that?"

"It wasn't me. It was God. God gave me the power to heal your daughter."

He hugs me. "God bless you!" He then hugs his daughter.

I smile, my heart filled with happiness. What a joy to bring joy to others! I can't wait to heal more children!

Abby looks at me with an incredulous look on her face. I can tell she is wondering whether to let me into the hospital. Am I safe?

"I'm just here to heal the kids," I say. I point to the media. "They'll be my witnesses."

"Okay," she says, reluctantly. "Come on. Let's go, then."

I follow Abby to the elevator. The media follows.

"That was fantastic," Kathy says as we step into the elevator. She raises her mic, and her photographer rolls on the impromptu interview. "How did you come to get these amazing powers?"

I shrug. "My guardian angel came to me in human form and told me God chose me before I was born to do this. My mission from God is to spread the message that God is real and loves all His creation."

"Wow, that's amazing," Kathy says.

The elevator opens to the cancer wing. Over the next few hours, I walk room to room and heal all the children I encounter. The camera crews get it all on tape. There are a lot of tears from parents and nurses as they watch me in awe heal one kid after another. Countless sick children rise from their beds and go home healthy. Eventually, the CEO of the hospital joins us.

"You're costing us a lot of money," he tells me with a laugh. "All our patients are leaving. At this rate, we won't have any patients to care for!"

"That's the goal," I chuckle. "I know you're in the business of healing people, but my way of healing them is faster – and cheaper."

"I appreciate you healing these kids. It's amazing this power you have. You're like Jesus."

"Please, don't compare me to Jesus."

“But you are like a modern-day Jesus. I’m okay losing money as long as these kids get to go home healthy.”

“I’m glad I can help.” Feeling tired and rundown, I say, “I need to get home and get some rest. Healing Is a tiresome business! But I’ll come back later to heal more kids.”

“Anytime,” he says.

I raise my staff. “Take me home!” The hospital dissipates and I am back in my living room. I see Anna sitting on the couch watching TV. It’s the news, talking about me and my miracles at Children’s Mercy.

“There you are!” Anna says. “It looks like you healed a lot of kids today. I saw it all on the news.”

“I did heal a lot of kids today. How are things here?”

“Crazy. Take a look out our front window.”

I walk over and look outside. Police have cordoned our street. I see a man in a dark sedan parked across the street. I assume he’s CIA. He is watching the thousands of people who have gathered outside our home. One group holds signs castigating me. The signs say things like, “Pretender. You’re the Anti-Christ” and “It’s Not God, But the Devil Leading This Sinner!” and “Killer! May God Strike You Down.” Another group sits in a circle, deep in prayer, holding signs that say, “God Sent This Prophet to Heal Us!” and “Christian is a True Christian!”. The media is also outside, getting video and interviews for later newscasts.

"We'll never have privacy now," I moan. "Did you pack our bags for the hotel."

"I did," Anna answers. I see our two bags sitting in the entryway. I grab one while Anna grabs the other. Anna then grabs my shirt with her free hand, and I say, "Take us to the Marriott downtown."

We teleport to the Marriott in downtown Kansas City. Since people now know my face, I ask Anna to go inside and get us a room with her fake ID and CIA credit card. I hide outside, not wanting to be seen. I'm already tired of the publicity. I don't like the attention. But what can I do? This is what God wants of me.

Anna returns with a room key.

"We don't need those. What room are we in?" I ask.

"Room 568."

I raise my staff as Anna grabs my shirt. "Take us to room 586."

I hear Anna say "No" as we appear in a room. I see a man and woman lying in bed, watching a movie on TV. They sit up in shock.

"What the... What are you doing in our room?"

"Sorry!" I say. "I meant, take us to Room 568."

We teleport to our empty room. Anna and I start laughing.

"Whoops," I say.

"Did you see the look on that man's face? He was in complete shock!"

"I feel bad."

"As you should! This is just more proof you never listen to me."

"I do listen. I just misheard you."

"Sure," Anna laughs as she sits on the bed. "Now what."

I lean the staff against the wall and say, "I need a break. This healing business is really tiring. Did you see all the people on our front lawn? I'm a little concerned how some don't believe I'm a prophet sent by God."

"You didn't think everyone would accept you as a prophet, did you?"

"Kind of," I say. "I mean, I'm doing things no one else can do. How can they not see these powers come from God?"

"Some will always think your powers come from the devil. I don't know if you'll be able to change their minds."

"I certainly have to try," I say. "Isn't that what God wants?"

"Of course, but convincing people you're not the devil will be tough."

CHAPTER 23

We order room service for dinner and turn the television on to the National Geographic channel. We are both excited to see the special on our trip and how Marcus and Eli put it all together. It's strange to see video of us camping on Mount Nebo, then blowing up the side of the mountain, then finding the Ark. We were just there yesterday and already, our journey is on TV for the whole world to see.

"And then, as they entered the cave, they came across the glittering, gold-covered Ark of the Covenant," the narrator says in a deep voice. "After lifting the lid, Christian Hagios, the leader of this expedition, grabbed a hold of the staff of Aaron from inside the Ark and discovered it possessed great powers. He soon learned how to harness those powers and teleported his colleague, Jermaine, and the Ark from Jordan back to a lab in Lawrence, Kansas, 6600 miles away. Thanks to the powers within the staff, they made the trip in the blink of an eye."

They then show the video the grad student recorded inside Jermaine's lab. The special also includes our interviews and other video of the Ark inside the cave. Overall, Marcus and Eli did a fantastic job putting it all together on such a tight deadline. I hoped everyone who watched the show would now be convinced of God's existence.

I turn off the TV and ask Anna, "What more should I do to draw people closer to God?"

"Hmmm. That's a good question. What does your gut tell you?"

"You mean, what does Mike say I should do next? Let me ask."

I close my eyes and put my hands together in prayer. I silently talk to Mike, asking for his guidance, and it doesn't take long before I hear his answer in my head.

"Mike says it's time for me to help people without any of the cameras around," I say. "He says it's time for me to do good for goods sake."

"But I thought God wanted the whole world to see His powers."

"He does. But He also wants me to show humbleness by helping people without getting attention." I look up. "Okay God, I am your servant. Send me where you must."

"Right now?" Anna asks.

"There's no time like the present," I say. "I'll be back before ten." I grab the staff and stand up. "God, please take me to someone who needs my help."

I suddenly appear in a back alley. It's dark, and I can hardly see. I notice a group of people – young teens – standing in a circle, hitting and kicking someone on the ground in the middle of them. I turn to them and yell, "Get away from him!"

They all stop and look at me. Every one of them smiles at me with an evil grin, and they all walk toward me. It's as if they are possessed by demons. I glance at the guy they were beating. He lies on the ground, moaning, unable to move. His face is covered with blood.

"You want some of this?" a young teen with a mohawk and tear tattoo near his right eye yells at me.

I wave the staff. An invisible force lifts him and everyone else in his group about five feet up into the air. I swing the staff and throw them against a nearby brick wall.

"What the... " the mohawked teen mutters as he slowly stands back up.

I lift my staff and throw him against the brick alley wall again. The entire group stands up and runs off.

I walk over to the man on the ground. "Are you okay?"

All he can do is moan. I lay my hand on his shoulder and close my eyes. "Lord, please heal him." Within seconds, the man's broken bones and bruised skin are healed.

"How did you do that?" he asks in wonderment.

"It wasn't me, but God who saved you," I say.

"Then thank you, God, for saving my life. They were going to kill me." He sits up. "Hey, I know you! You're the guy on the news! The one who claims to have God's powers. And you used them to save me?"

"I did," I say.

"Wow! Thank you."

"Are you okay? Should I call for a paramedic?"

He looks at himself. Satisfied he's healthy enough to stand up and walk home without assistance, he says, "No, I'm okay."

"Great. I'm going to help someone else now. Stay safe!"

I wonder what God has in store for me next. Taking me to a beating was quite a surprise. I stand up, grip the staff and say, "Lord, take me to someone else who needs my help."

I now stand in a dark basement. I blink to adjust my eyes to the darkness. Impatient, I say, "Lord, light up this room." The end of my staff glows. I scan the room and see a teenaged girl chained to a pole. The room smells of feces and spoiled food. A tray of moldy food sits near her feet. The girl's hair is matted. Her jeans and flannel shirt are torn and filthy. I notice dried blood around her wrists, underneath restraints. She's pulled on them to try and break free. I am not mentally prepared to see this. Who is this girl and why is she chained up? She stares at me with bewilderment.

"What's going on here?" I whisper, worried someone upstairs might hear us and come downstairs.

"Who are you?" she whispers harshly.

"My name is Christian. God sent me here to save you."

"Can you get me out of these handcuffs?" she asks.

"Of course." I raise my staff. "Lord, please free this young woman."

The handcuffs unlock and fall to the ground. The girl rubs her wrists and stands up.

"Who did this to you?" I ask.

"My mom and dad. I talked back to them, so they locked me up in the basement."

"Do they do this often?"

She nods. I see a tear fall down her cheek.

The basement door opens. I hear a harsh, rough voice echo throughout the room.

"Nora? What's going on down there? Why is there a light on? Honey, did you turn on a light for Nora?"

"Of course not!" a woman says in a shrill, angry voice. I assume that is her mother.

I hear heavy footsteps on the stairs. A gruff-looking man with a long beard and beady eyes enters the basement and stares at me. "Who are… wait. I know you. I seen you on the news!"

"What's going on here?" I ask as I point to the teenaged girl, who is still standing by the pole where she had been chained.

"None of your God-damn business. You need to get the hell out of my house!" he yells. "Nora, come here!" The girl slinks over to his side. I see him reach behind his back and pull out a gun.

As he points it toward me, I yell, "Get that gun out of his hand!" The gun suddenly becomes scalding hot and turns orange. The man drops the gun, and it quickly melts into a small pool of metal.

"Ouch! You burned me!"

"What are you doing to this girl?" I ask.

He sneers, and I swear I see Lucifer standing in the shadows behind him. Calmly, he says, "Like I said, it's none of your God-damn business. Leave! Now!"

He slowly reaches to his side and pulls out a long knife from a leather sheath. The metal gleams by the light of my staff.

"What don't you understand," I say in frustration. "Heat up the knife, too, please."

His knife suddenly glows orange and he drops it while screaming in pain. He grabs his burnt hand and blows on it.

"I'm done playing games with you," I say. "What you're doing to your daughter is criminal. Nora, come to me and I will take you to the police."

She grabs her father's arm. "No, I want to stay here?"

"But he chained you up."

"I don't care. He's my dad," she answers.

I don't understand but remember reading how some crime victims bond with their oppressors. But still, I can't leave her here with this monster. I'm confused about what I should do. Didn't God send me here to save her? And yet, she doesn't want to be saved.

A voice in my head says, 'Go get the police.' Is that Mike talking to me again? His message makes sense. But then again, I don't even know what city I'm in. Or state. Or country. All I know is I'm in a basement somewhere in the world and need to save this girl.

I grip the staff and say, "Take me outside this house."

It is night. I am standing on the front lawn of a ranch-style home under serious disrepair. Paint peels from the outside walls, the tiles on the roof are worn off, and there is trash piled up on the front lawn. I look at the number on the house and glance at the street name. I commit it to memory and say, "Take me to the closest police station."

I am now standing outside a police substation. A sign nearby reads, "Cleveland Police Department." I walk inside and the female sergeant behind a glass window recognizes me.

"Are you kidding me? You? I just saw you on TV healing a bunch of kids!"

"Hi, I'm Christian Hagios. I want to report a crime."

"You do?" she asks.

"Yes, there is a girl handcuffed in her basement not far from here. The address is 10402 Highland Street. Can you send over some officers to save her?"

The woman looks confused. "How do you know this?"

"God took me there. With my staff. Please, for the girl's sake, send officers over there. Her father has her locked up in the basement."

"Okay," she says. "I'll send officers to that address." She smiles. "I can't believe you're here!"

"Sorry, but I have to go help someone else now," I say. I grip my staff and say, "Lord, please take me to someone else who needs help."

The inside of the police station disappears. I am now standing outside a burning house. Flames lick the dark sky as firefighters pull their hoses and spray water on the house. I hear a man screaming behind me.

"My son is still in there!"

An overweight Hispanic man tries to run toward the flames, but a firefighter grabs him and holds him back. No one notices my arrival amid the chaos of the moment. I feel practically invisible.

"Stop, sir," the firefighter says to the father. "Where is he?"

"My son is in the basement!" he yells.

Without thinking, I say, "Take me to this man's son!"

I am now standing inside a glowing orange room with flames all around me. The air is thick with black smoke. I cough as smoke fills my lungs. The heat inside the burning room warms my skin. The sound of burning wood crackles in my ears. I see a young man passed out on the floor. I run over, kneel, and put my left hand on his back.

"Take us outside!" I say.

We are now outside. I suck in the fresh air and look for the boy's father. He sees us and runs over with tears in his eyes. He drops next to his son and shakes him. "Jose. Jose. Wake up!"

I see Jose is not breathing, so I say, "Let Jose breathe again." Jose inhales deeply and begins to cough.

"Jose! You're alive! Are you okay?"

Jose slowly rolls over on his back and with his eyes still closed, says, "I'm alive, Papa. Thanks to God."

Jose's father looks up at me. "I can't believe it. Are you an angel?"

I shake my head. "I'm a prophet from God," I say.

"You saved my son's life. Thank you!"

"Of course!" I say. "I'm glad I could help."

"But... but how?"

I lift my staff. "God granted me powers to help people like your son. I'm glad I could be here to save him." I stand up as paramedics rush over to Jose's side. They ignore me and put their focus on Jose.

I feel completely exhausted. I only saved three people, but it feels like 300. I know there are many more people in need of saving, but I can't help anyone else right now. I need a break. I feel like I'm disappointing God and tear up. This experience shows me how this world is so broken! There is so much tragedy! So many people in need of help!

"Take me back to Anna," I say.

I am back in our hotel room. Anna lies in bed and jerks upright when I appear.

"I don't think I'll ever get used to you just showing up like that," she laughs. She gives me a look of concern. "Oh my, Chris. You have ash all over your face. Are you okay?"

I sigh and lean my staff against the wall before sitting down on the bed. I begin to cry. I can't help it. Anna gets out of the covers and slides over to give me a hug.

"What's wrong, honey? Wow, you really smell like smoke."

"I don't know," I say. "So many people need my help. It's so overwhelming!"

"I bet," she answers. "But God doesn't expect you to save everyone, right? You can only do so much. How many people did you save tonight?"

"Three. But that doesn't seem like nearly enough."

"Do you want to go out and help some more people?"

I shake my head. "Not tonight. I'm exhausted. And it was scary. Some people tried to kill me."

"They did?" Anna asks.

"I also saved a young man from a burning house."

"Wow! That's intense."

"It really was. I think it'll be best if I get some sleep and try again tomorrow.

"Okay, let's put you to bed," Anna says.

I can't even muster enough energy to wash my face. I fall back onto the hotel bed with my clothes still on and fall asleep as soon as my head hits the pillow.

CHAPTER 24

I wake up refreshed. My energy is replenished. I feel like I'm starting to better process my current situation. So much has happened over the past few days. I discovered the fabled Ark of the Covenant, met the President of the United States, killed Russia's president, went on national television, healed a bunch of children, and saved three people from dangerous situations. What would today bring? I had an idea to run past Anna.

I look over and Anna is awake, smiling at me.

"Good morning," she says.

"Good morning to you," I reply. "I want to run something by you."

"Go ahead," she says as she sits up in bed. Her natural beauty and inner warmth continues to fascinate me, and I realize how lucky I am to be with her.

"What if I did a public healing outside Union Station."

"A public healing?"

"What if I invite everyone in the city to come to Union Station to witness God's powers in a public setting. Kind of like Jesus did when he gave his sermon on the mountain."

"You mean the Sermon on the Mount?"

"Yeah, that. It's a way to show God's power to a large group of people in a public setting."

"But why Union Station?"

"Because that's where we host rallies when the Chiefs and Royals win Super Bowls and World Series."

"But wasn't there a shooting there a few years ago?"

"I'll use God's powers to prevent something like that from happening again," I say. "What do you think?"

Anna contemplates my suggestion. "I suppose it would be a terrific opportunity to share God's powers and message with a lot of people. But I can't help but worry. That CIA agent warned us to stay hidden. If you do this, you'll be out in the open for anyone who wants to hurt you."

I pull out the phone the CIA agent gave me from my suitcase. "I'll call him and let him know, so he can have agents there to protect us. Plus, I have my staff to protect us."

"Can you really get it all organized this quickly?"

"Let me get the ball rolling."

I pull out reporter Kathy Bergstrom's business card out of my front pocket and call her with my CIA burner phone.

"This is Kathy."

"Kathy. Christian Hagios."

"Christian?" I hear an alertness in her voice. "How can I help you?"

"Can you help me with something?" I tell her my plan to heal people and ask if she can get Union Station to set up a stage out front for me for later that day.

"That's a quick turnaround," she says.

"I know, but it needs to be quick. Tell your Union Station contacts and the rest of the city I will be there at four o'clock today. If anyone wants to be healed, have them gather near the front of the stage."

"But I'm just a reporter."

"A reporter with contacts who trust you. Tell them I'll be there at four, and whatever happens, happens. If there's no stage, there's no stage. But I'll be at Union Station at four o'clock today to heal whoever needs healing."

"Okay, I'll reach out to my people at Union Station and let them know," Kathy says. "I'll get the word out on the news, too."

"Thank you." I hang up and turn to Anna. "Hopefully she can get it all organized."

"What's the rush?" Anna asks.

"I feel like God is going to take His powers away from me soon."

"Really? Why?"

"It's just a feeling I have. In my gut. I don't think God wants me to have His powers forever. Just long enough to make a difference."

"Interesting."

"I need to do as much as I can right now with God's powers. I can't wait until later."

"Okay. Mike did tell you to trust your gut."

"That's what my gut is telling me. Also, I have a crazy proposition."

"What's that?"

"What if I went and visited the Pope."

"The Pope?"

"Yeah. Maybe pick his brain. See what he thinks about all of this."

Anna laughs. "I mean, it's a crazy proposition. But why not? You have the means." She nods toward the staff leaning against the wall. "However, you need to look presentable if you're going to do that. You need to take a shower and wear something nice."

I shower and wash the ash off me while Anna orders room service for breakfast. Anna packed all my toiletries, so when I get out of the shower, I brush my teeth and shave. When I walk out of the bathroom with a towel around my waist, a plate of scrambled eggs, hashbrowns, bacon, and toast is waiting for me.

"What are you going to wear?" Anna asks. Anna didn't pack anything other than jeans and polo shirts.

"A suit?" I ask. Anna nods. I grab the staff and say, "God, please put me in a nice suit."

It's the strangest feeling, going from naked to wearing a suit. The towel drops to the ground as a black suit magically appears over my body. I look in the mirror and see the suit comes with a purple tie. It all fits me perfectly. There's even a purple pocket square in the outer pocket of my suit jacket.

"Wow, you clean up good," Anna says as she sits on the bed, finishing up her breakfast of granola and fruit.

"Think this will work?" I ask.

"It will."

I sit down and eat my breakfast. Afterwards, I grab the staff from the wall. "Wish me luck."

"Good luck," she says.

I grip the staff and say, "God, please take me to the Pope."

I am now standing in an ornate room in Vatican City. Beautiful, religious oil paintings and white marble statues decorate the room. The architecture is unlike anything I've ever seen, with gold molding separating the ceiling into different sections. Each section is decorated with a different religious scene, painted in bright oil paints. The Pope wears a white outfit and sits behind a massive desk, looking at paperwork. He is alone. He looks up in shock.

"Di dove sei?" he asks.

"Do you speak English?" I ask.

He does. "Where did you come from?" he asks.

"Do you know who I am?" I ask.

The Pope nods.

"May I sit?"

The Pope nods. I sit across from him.

"Can I ask you some questions?" I ask.

He nods again.

"You are obviously closer to God than anyone else in the world, and God wants me to bring people closer to Him, but I'm not a pastor. I'm not you. I'm just a normal person. I don't know how to do it. What should I tell the people?"

"Are you… " He stops abruptly and clears his throat. "Are you Catholic, young man?"

"Catholic? No. Why?"

"I cannot help you."

"I'm sorry, what?"

"Please, young man, don't try to fool me like you have fooled the rest of the world. We both know the truth. All of this is a hoax. Yes, you are an incredibly talented magician, and if you are doing these tricks to get more people to come to God, then good for you. But honestly, all your work is in vain unless you and the rest of the people turn to Catholicism."

"Why do you say that?"

"Catholicism is the only true path to God. All other religions are pretenders."

"Seriously?" I feel my voice get louder and my blood pressure rise. "I just appeared in your office holding the staff of Aaron, and you think I'm a pretender? I'm sorry for getting angry, but I'm not Catholic and yet God gave me these powers. If you reject me, you are, in fact, rejecting God."

"I disagree. I do not believe God gave His powers to a non-believer from America. Your claims are absurd and frankly, they're sacrilegious."

"I'm not as well-versed in the Bible as you are, but you should know better than anyone how God often chooses those you least expect to spread His Word. I mean, come one! Jesus hung out with sinners, right? And he was killed for it."

"Surely you are not comparing yourself to Jesus."

"No, not at all. I am a prophet, not the Son of God. But I must tell you, being Catholic is not a prerequisite to getting into heaven."

The Pope lifts his chin at me. "Of course it is."

"The Archangel Michael says otherwise."

The Pope's eye narrow. "You spoke with the Archangel Michael?"

"He's my guardian angel. He's the one who told me that all who believe in God, no matter what religion, will go to heaven, because God created all humans and loves them all. We all just worship God in different ways. But it doesn't mean you're right and I'm wrong. Michael told me the path to heaven is through accepting all people, loving them, and helping those in need."

The Pope waves his hand at me. "That is quite the story. But I still don't believe you."

An idea pops in my head. "Let me show you the truth behind what I say. Would you like to see the Ark of the Covenant?"

"Of course."

"Then let's go."

"Now?"

"Yes," I smile. I walk behind the desk and the Pope stands. I put my hand on his shoulder. "God, please take us to the Ark of the Covenant."

We are now standing in Jermaine's lab in Lawrence, Kansas. The golden Ark sits on a large table to our left. The two versions of the Ten Commandments also sit on the table. The broken tablet has been pieced back together in their original form, like a jigsaw puzzle. The Pope stares at the Ark with an incredulous look on his face.

"Go ahead and touch it, if you'd like," I say. "It won't hurt you."

The Pope slowly raises his hand, makes the sign of the cross, and touches the Ark. He looks at me and smiles. "It's cold." He traces the outside and looks inside. He then steps over to the Ten Commandment and touches the carvings. "Thou shalt have no other God before me."

"Is that what it says?" I ask.

"The first commandment, yes. It is written in Aramaic. A dead language now. But I know a little of it."

"Wow," is all I can say as I watch the Pope examine the relics. This is surreal, being with the Pope in my friend's lab in Kansas.

The Pope looks at me. "If you give me these artifacts, I will ensure they are on public display for all time."

"I'm sorry, but I've already promised them to the Smithsonian. Maybe after their contract with Jordan ends."

"How long from now?"

"Ten years."

The Pope nods. "Okay. I will wait. But please arrange for it to come to Vatican City next, yes?"

"I will try my best," I say. "Do you now believe I am a prophet of God?"

The Pope nods and makes the sign of the cross. “I am sorry I doubted you. Only God could take me from my office in Vatican City to America to see His Glorious Ark of the Covenant. May I pray over you?”

“Please,” I say as I lean the staff against my body, clasp my hands and bow my head. I feel the Pope’s hand touch my shoulder.

“Dear Lord, please be with Christian as he spreads your word to the masses. Protect him and open the ears and hearts of all to turn toward you. Guide his speech to convince others to accept your love and grace in their hearts. In your name we pray, Amen.”

The Pope then makes the sign of the cross, gets on his knees, reaches out to touch the Ark, and begins to say a prayer in Latin. When he finishes, he stands and says, “All right. I’m ready to go back to my office.”

I touch his white cloak, grip my staff, and say, “God, please take us back to the Pope’s office.”

We are now once again standing next to his desk. The Pope sits down and motions for me to go to the other side and sit in a guest chair, which I do.

“I will be honest. I am still struggling with all you say about how all those who believe in God go to heaven. Not just good Catholics,” the Pope says.

I lean back. “It seems to be a trend in religion, where the leaders of different faiths tell their followers the only way to heaven is by believing everything they say. But where you go after death is not based on what you believe, but more so on how you live.”

“But what you say goes against the very fabric of Christianity. As written in John, 14:6, “Jesus said to him, 'I am the way, and the truth, and the life. No one comes to the Father except through me.'"

I shrug. “I’m just telling you what the Archangel Michael told me. Who am I to doubt an angel?”

The Pope shakes his head. “You have been gifted an incredible honor by God to influence humanity in such a way. You have a great responsibility to do good. You said you aren’t a religious man?”

“I am now. But before finding the Ark? I wasn’t that religious. Honestly, I don’t know why God chose me.”

“God seems to enjoy making the ordinary, extraordinary. Like He did with David. From shepherd to king. Belief in God, though, is always the most important quality of a prophet. You now believe in God?”

“I do. Without a doubt.”

“Then keep sharing your story. Be honest. Tell others how you used to doubt God and how our Savior opened your eyes to the truth. My advisors tell me you’ve been healing the sick?”

“Some.”

“Do more. Show the world God’s powers and give all glory to God. That is how you bring people closer to our Creator.”

“I will. Thank you.”

“I believe our time is up. I have much important work to do.”

I bid the Pope goodbye, grab my staff, and return to Anna in our hotel room. She is on the bed, working on her computer. Startled, she puts her computer aside, gets up, and gives me a hug and kiss.

“Welcome back. How’s the Pope?”

“He’s good,” I say nonchalantly, as if seeing the Pope is an everyday occurrence. I lean my staff against the wall. “He gave me some great advice.”

“What’s that.”

“Just to be honest when it comes to my beliefs. To tell others I doubted the existence of God before but don’t anymore.”

“That sounds like great advice.”

“What have you been doing?”

Anna frowns. "I've been reading stories about you online. On my computer."

"Oh, oh. Not good?"

Anna shakes her head. "There is still so much doubt out there. Now some experts are claiming you planted a bunch of healthy kids at the hospital, paid them to pretend to be sick, and then pretended to heal them."

"What? Surely the doctors confirmed these kids I healed were truly sick."

"The doctors couldn't confirm anything due to HIPPA laws. These stories I'm reading are so one-sided."

"What else?"

"A lot of religious publications are questioning whether you are truly talking to God or if Satan is simply using you to turn people toward evil. The say you're pretending to talk to God to trick others into sin."

"What? Ugh!" I sit on the bed, defeated. "Now I know how Jesus felt when everyone turned against him."

"Let's just hope your story doesn't end the same way as his."

"I'd rather not be nailed to a cross. However, I understand now why God decided to send a prophet. I'm healing people and yet, some people don't want to believe God is behind all of it. How frustrating for God! All these people He created continue to doubt His existence even though I'm giving them a ton of proof God exists. Why are people so stubborn? Why are they so naïve? Why won't they just open their hearts and believe in a higher being who created them?"

"Because changing their belief system scares them," Anna says. "Some people have spent their whole lives doubting the existence of God. Or believing something different from what you're now preaching. To change their beliefs would destroy everything they've thought is true up to this point in their lives."

"If I saw someone else performing all these miracles and said God gave them these powers, I would believe that person right away."

"Would you though? I mean, you were a pretty stubborn atheist until Mike showed up."

I smile. "You're right. Maybe I would still doubt. A little. That's why I think healing people outside Union Station in a public setting will help convince even more people that I am speaking the truth about God. When I heal people, they'll see it's not a magic trick but due to the power of God."

Anna grabs the remote and turns on the TV. "By the way, they're already at Union Station." She turns to a local news channel. The picture shows a mass of people gathered outside Union Station. People are sitting on blankets. Some hold signs. Some proclaim me to be Satan. Others, the second coming of

Jesus. The lower graphic reads, "Prophet to Address Kansas City Crowd at Four O'clock". I ask Anna to turn up the volume as Kathy Bergstrom previews my appearance.

"We are still four hours away from Christian Hagios arriving here, and already, the space outside Union Station is packed with people. Crews are setting up the stage right now. We will be live once he arrives, so don't turn the channel. I spoke to Union Station officials, and they told me they are more than happy to host this event. Kansas City police tell me they will have extra officers here to make sure everyone stays safe. They want to make sure we don't have another shooting in this area, like what happened back in 2024 during the Chief's Super Bowl rally here."

They go back to the anchor in the studio. "Kathy, do you have any idea what to expect when Christian arrives?"

They go back to Kathy. There are people with signs standing behind her. "He told me he would be here at four o'clock and plans to heal a bunch of people. He wants to show the world God exists. We'll have to wait and see what happens when he arrives, but one thing is for sure: whether you believe in God or not, Union Station will be the place to be today."

"Yes, it will be," the anchor says as the news goes back to the studio.

The anchor goes to the next story. "This just in, the Vatican is reporting that Christian Hagios visited the Pope a few minutes ago. They say he, uh, teleported the Pope to the University of Kansas to see the Ark of the Covenant. That's a sentence I never thought I'd say. Hagios and a group of archeologists recovered the Ark yesterday at Mount Nebo, Jordan.

"In other news, we're getting word that the world's cache of nuclear weapons has indeed been turned into paper airplanes, as Hagios said he would do last night on..."

Anna turns off the TV.

"Wow, news travels fast," Anna says.

"I just got back from the Vatican and it's already on the news?"

Anna looks at her watch. "We have four hours before we need to be at Union Station. What do you want to do this afternoon?"

"I should go help more people, but honestly, I'm tired. I'd love to just snuggle in bed with you and nap."

"Let's do that!" Anna smiles.

"What do you want for lunch?"

"A turkey sandwich sounds good right now."

I raise the staff and say, "God, please send us two turkey sandwiches with fries."

Two plates suddenly appear on a nearby counter. There are two sandwiches and fries sitting on them.

"Lunch is served," I say.

"I could get used to this!" Anna says as she walks over and grabs both plates.

I take off my suit and put on my pajamas. I sit on the bed next to Anna and eat my lunch. Afterwards, I put both plates on the ground, and we lay down in bed. Within minutes, we are both asleep, resting in preparation for the exhaustive work ahead of us.

CHAPTER 25

"You'll be by my side the whole time?" I ask Anna as we sit up in bed and shake off the drowsiness from our afternoon nap.

"Of course! I'm not crazy about the attention, but I think it's important the world see I'm supporting you in all of this. Who am I to deny God? He chose you, which means He also chose me."

I get out of bed and ask God for a change of clothes. A pair of jeans and a plain, gray sweatshirt replace my pajamas. Anna changes into an outfit she brought from home, also jeans and a sweatshirt.

"Ready?" I ask Anna.

She walks over to me and grabs my arm "Ready."

"All right. God, please take us to the stage in front of Union Station."

We now are standing on a large stage in front of Union Station, the iconic Kansas City train station. As always, I'm a little disoriented with my sudden arrival at a new place. I scan the massive crowd in front of me. They take up the entire parking lot, street, and lawn on either side of the building. The crowd fills the entire hill in front of me leading up to the World War I Museum. I'm impressed that so many people showed up.

We hear a huge roar as the crowd stands and claps on our arrival. Many are pointing at us. The sound of thousands of people chatting with excitement fills the air. I feel like a rock star at a stadium concert. My guess? There are more than a million people here.

I notice a line of police officers in front of the stage, keeping people from jumping up and mobbing us. In front of the officers is a line of cameras, representing both local and national media outlets. Massive TV screens on either side magnify Anna and me for all to see. The Union Station folks thought of everything. I also notice agents in black suits scattered throughout the crowd. I assume they are CIA, keeping watch to keep me safe. I look at Anna, and she exhales loudly.

"Wow, what a crowd," she says.

"It feels like we're at a Taylor Swift concert," I say.

"If only you could sing."

The people near the front push closer to the stage. A middle-aged man with a gray beard and long hair breaks through and tries to climb onto the stage. An officer pulls him down and puts him in handcuffs. I walk to the edge of the stage. The man looks at me with tears. "Please! My wife has cancer. Please heal her!"

I see an older woman with gray hair walk over to him. She looks up at me with sad eyes.

"Come here." The woman approaches me at the edge of the stage. "What's your name?"

"Caroline."

"Caroline, do you believe in God?"

"I do!"

I jump down to the ground, grip my staff, and touch her shoulder. I close my eyes and bow my head. "By the power granted to me by God, I order the cancer to leave your body!"

Caroline suddenly faints. The officer arresting her husband catches her. She quickly awakens in his arms.

"What... what happened?"

I smile. "God just took the cancer out of your body. You're healed?"

"Really?" she asks with joy as she stands up on her own. She turns to her husband. "Can you believe it?"

"I certainly want to. Thank you."

I ask the officer to let him go, and they leave holding hands.

"Can I go next!" I hear someone in the crowd scream.

I see stairs off to my right. I raise my staff to the crowd in front of me and they become silent.

"I want to heal all of you. But on the stage, so the whole world can see God's greatness." I walk over to the stairs and go back on the stage. I see the Union Station staff gathered nearby. They all wear polo shirts with the Union Station logo on them.

"Thank you for all this," I say to them. "Can you please help me control the crowd and have the people come on stage one at a time?" The staff nods and jumps into action. They ask everyone who wants to be healed to form a single-file line.

I see a microphone and sound system nearby. I grab the microphone and turn it on.

"Testing, 1, 2, 3," I say into the mic. My voice carries into the crowd. "Attention, everyone." The crowd goes silent. "Hi. My name is Christian Hagios. This is my wife, Anna. I want to tell you my story."

I tell everyone about our son's suicide, my doubts about God, the visit from my guardian angel, how God chose me to be His prophet, how my guardian angel led us to the Ark of the Covenant, and how God wants me to use the staff to perform miracles. I also apologize for the death of Russia's president and promised to use God's powers for good. I explain how I want to use His powers to heal people, and I want the whole world to see.

"By the way," I say, "I did not ask for these powers. I did not ask for this responsibility. But when God calls on you, what choice do you have? God chose me for some odd reason, so here I am. Talking to all of you, right now. In this moment.

"I want all of you to know that God is real. Heaven is real. Your doubt doesn't change the truth. Seeing God's powers work through me should be proof enough. Also, I tell you this with His authority. God loves you. All of you. God wants you to live a good life. To be a good human. To help others in need. So, quit being selfish. Quit hurting others. Quit putting wealth, power, and vanity ahead of God. Love your neighbor, use your God-given talents to help others, and make this world a better place." I'm impressed with myself but know the Holy Spirit gave me the words the people need to hear.

There is a smattering of applause from those who support me and believe I am truly a prophet of God. Many others don't clap but stare at me with a strange look of disgust and fascination on their faces.

I look over at the stairs to my right and nod to the Union staff member controlling the line.

"Go ahead and send me the first person who needs healing," I say into the microphone.

The staff member grips the arm of a blind man and helps him step up on stage. He taps a long white cane on the ground to know what's in front of him. Anna walks over to him, greets him, and gently leads him to me.

"What's your name and what would you like me to do today?" I say into the microphone.

"My name is..." He flinches hearing his voice echo over the loudspeaker. "My name is Vance Jewett. I am from Kansas City, Missouri, and I'm hoping you can help me see again."

"How long have you been blind?" I ask.

"My whole life. I was born with a rare eye condition and have never been able to see."

"Are you here alone or did you come with family and friends?"

"My family is here."

"We love you, Vance!" I hear someone screaming from the front. I find them in the crowd and wave.

"Who is here with you?" I ask.

"My parents."

I wave them over and have them come on stage. They join us, hug their son, and then turn their attention toward me.

"Can you confirm to the crowd your son was born blind?"

"We can," his father says as he leans into the mic.

"Have you tried any surgeries or medicine to regain his eyesight."

His dad leans into the mic again. "We have. But nothing has worked."

"All right. Back up, please."

Vance's parents move behind us. I hand the mic to Anna, place my left hand over Vance's eyes, close my eyes, grip my staff, and say, "God, please let Vance Jewett see."

"Oh my God!"

I open my eyes and see Vance looking at me with wide eyes. "I can see you!"

I smile. Seeing joy on the faces of the people I help never gets old.

"You can?" I ask.

"Yes!" Vance looks out into the crowd. "Wow." He then looks back at his parents. "Mom? Dad?" They cry and hug. Anna gives me back the mic and leads Vance and his parents off the opposite end of the stage.

"Who's next?" I ask.

I hear a disturbing chant as a man with a megaphone starts screaming at me. All the people around him repeat what he says.

"Christian is a fake… He's an insult to God… Pretending to have God's powers… He's going to hell!" The man with the megaphone repeats it and each time, more people in the crowd join in.

I try to ignore them, but it still hurts my heart. I just healed a blind man. They all saw it! How can they be so blind? Why do they refuse to believe in the miracle they just witnessed? Why do they continue to think I'm a fake? An imposter? A magician? Why do they refuse to believe God made me his prophet?

Then it dawns on me. People are so used to being duped by those in power. It's easy to doubt. It's easier to believe I'm a fake rather than believe God gave me His powers.

A woman carrying a baby walks on stage.

"What's your name and why are you here?" I ask into the microphone, speaking over the crowd's chants.

Their hateful words distract the woman as she looks at them with concern on her face. Then she returns her attention to me.

"Uh, my name is… sorry, my name is Lisa McDonald. I drove in from St. Louis to meet you. This is my daughter, Rebecca. She has end stage kidney disease. I'm hoping you can cure her."

I hand the mic to Anna, put my hand on Rebecca's forehead, and say, "God, please heal Rebecca." Her baby suddenly kicks and squirms. Lisa's face lights up.

"I can't believe it! She hardly moves because of her condition but look at her now! Thank you!"

Anna hands me the microphone and walks Lisa off stage. I turn to the crowd, getting more annoyed by all the negative chants.

"If you don't want to believe God gave me His powers, then maybe you should just leave," I say. "You're being disruptive and rude. Let me heal these people in peace."

More shouts came my way along with a smattering of boos.

"Faker!"

"You're the anti-Christ!"

"You can't fool us!"

"Poser!"

"Next!" I say, determined to prove them wrong. A teenaged boy with a pigeon-toed walk and arms seemingly glued to his chest walks toward me. He wears glasses and struggles to speak.

"Hi. My name is Mark, and I have cerebral palsy. Can you help me?"

"Of course," I say. I hand the mic to Anna once again and put my left hand on his head. "God, please heal Mark."

Mark's legs and arms suddenly straighten. He looks down at them in awe.

"Wow!" he says with a normal sounding voice. It catches him by surprise. He flinches and starts to laugh. He then grabs the mic from Anna.

"People, I had cerebral palsy and Christian just healed me. It's a miracle! It could've only come from God!"

The boos get louder as some scream, "Get that actor off the stage!"

"He's faking it!"

"You're both an insult to God!"

Their faces turn red as they scream. Spit flies out of their mouths. They point at us and yell with such fury, they seem to be jumping out of their skin. I feel like the crowd is getting rowdier, and I can't control it. I wonder if healing others in public was a bad idea.

Mark looks at me with a sad face and gives me the mic.

"I tried," he says. "Thank you for healing me."

"Of course," I say with a smile. This is why I am here. This is my purpose, whether the crowd appreciates it or not.

I look out and see a crowd of believers who support me. It makes me smile, seeing their signs. They read, "Christian is a modern-day prophet!" and "God works in mysterious ways" and "Don't doubt – God is real!" I appreciate their support, but they are quiet and stand off to the side, unwilling to confront the doubters.

"Next!" I say.

I hear a gunshot. I feel a sharp pain in my chest. I look down and see blood staining my sweatshirt. There's a hole where the bullet entered my chest. I feel faint and nearly let go of the staff in shock.

"Heal me!" I gasp.

I look down and to my amazement, the bullet pushes out of my skin. It drops on the stage with a ping. My skin comes together and heals right before my eyes. The blood stops flowing. The pain evaporates. With the microphone still in my hand, I touch my chest where I saw a hole just seconds ago. Warm blood stains my fingertips. I wipe the blood on my pants. I'm in shock. Did someone just try to kill me? Who? Where? Why? Is Anna in danger?

I scan the crowd for the shooter. I look up at the Liberty Memorial, a tall tower on top of the World War I Museum, which stands in front of me. In the distance, I see a man running on the terrace. He carries a rifle. I point and put the mic to my mouth.

"Up there! There's the man who shot me!"

The police near me cannot get to him. I fear he's going to escape.

I raise my staff and say, "Bring that gunman to me!"

The shooter suddenly appears in front of me, holding his rifle. I quickly swing my staff down on his hands and knock the rifle to the ground. The gunman stands frozen in shock, confused as to how he went from running on the terrace to standing in front of the man he shot. The fact I wasn't dead confused him even more.

"Officers, grab the shooter!"

The man gathers his wits and spits on my chest. He starts screaming in Russian.

Russian?

"God, help me understand what he is saying." I ask.

I suddenly understand his Russian. "I kill you because you kill my president. And yet, you don't die? How come? You use magic powers to heal yourself. Powers from the devil! You are evil! You must die!"

I stare into his eyes and in perfect Russian, I say, "God gave me these powers, not the devil. I apologized for killing your president. It was an accident."

"Your apology is not good enough! Your apology won't bring him back."

A group of officers are now on stage. They pick up the rifle and put the shooter in handcuffs. As they leave, I see a hole in security. Where the officers once stood is quickly replaced by the group of people yelling at me and calling me a fraud.

I step back and take a deep breath. Should I continue to heal people? Should Anna and I leave? I still feel the need to convince the doubters that God is real. I haven't done enough yet. I haven't healed enough people. I decide to stay a little longer. If things head south, Anna and I can always leave.

"Are you okay?" Anna asks as she steps in close to me. She looks horrified by what just happened. She touches my bloody shirt. "You've been shot!"

"But I healed myself," I say.

"I don't care, Chris. Someone just tried to kill you!" Her eyes are filled with tears. "Maybe we should go. Now. This place is becoming too dangerous."

"The gunman is gone," I say as I shake my head. "We can't leave. I need to heal more people. No one said this would be easy. I need to stay. For now. Too many people still doubt God's powers."

"Okay, but let's not stay here too long," Anna says. "I don't like the way that group of people is yelling at you."

"We won't stay much longer," I say. I turn to the stairs. "Who's next?"

A man in his thirties wearing nice slacks and a polo shirt walks on stage toward me. On the surface, nothing seems to be wrong with him.

"What is your name and why are you here?" I ask.

"My name is Rod, and I need some money!"

I flinch. "I'm sorry. What?"

"Can you get me some money? With your powers, can you make money appear?"

"No! I'm not here to make you money. God wants me to heal people. Are you sick?"

"No," Rod says. "I'm just broke and thought you could make me some money."

"Leave." I point to the opposite end of the stage and a Union Station staff member leads him off.

Another young man wearing nice clothes comes on stage and approaches me. He grabs the mic from me before I can say anything.

"Hi, Christian. Hi, Kansas City. My mom is about to lose her home. Can you pay off her mortgage?"

"What? No."

"Can you at least make a new car appear for me?"

"A new car? Get off the stage!"

The man drops the mic and grabs Aaron's rod. He pulls it out of my hand and immediately falls to the ground, dead.

"You killed him!" someone in the audience screams.

I lean down, pick up the staff, touch his arm, and say, "God, please bring him back to life!"

The man opens his eyes and looks up at me with a terror. He quickly stands up and runs off stage, staring at me with fear on his face.

"You tried to kill me!" he screams as he walks down the stairs.

The crowd near me yells at me with anger and rage. They start to shake the stage. A couple of people climb up. I grab the mic and run over to Anna. I stand between her and the crowd.

"Get away from the stage" I yell as I swing the staff.

An invisible force lifts all the people in front of the stage into the air and throws them backwards thirty feet. Many of them land on the hard pavement. Some land on other people. Some are hurt and begin to cry. An officer nearby looks at me with anger. I notice the cameras are rolling, capturing everything. A roar rises from the crowd. People are screaming at me. Pointing. Their faces are distorted with anger.

"God would never hurt His people like you are right now!"

"You're the devil! Only the devil would hurt us!"

"Who are you going to kill next?"

"I'm sorry. It was an accident," I say into the mic.

The crowd continues to hurl insults at me. Some start throwing objects at me on stage. Rocks. Bottles. Food. I step back to avoid getting hit. While my instinct tells me it's time to go, I let my anger get the best of me.

"Don't you get it!" I scream into the mic. "I never wanted any of this! God chose me! Why can't you all get that through your thick skulls!"

I look at Anna.

"Let's go," she says.

I start to cry.

I can't help it. I feel like such a failure. I set up this rally to explain my story and turn people toward God, but now everyone is turning against me. They call me evil and fake. Another burst of anger boils over my soul. Why are the people still denying me? I want to help, and yet they refuse to accept the fact God sent me.

I am full of fury. Tears run down my cheeks as I step forward and yell, "You don't deserve this."

I drop the mic and raise my staff. The entire crowd boos. They continue to throw things at me. A rock hits my leg. Don't they know I could kill them all with one word? Don't they see all the good I could do if they would just support me?

"You don't deserve this!" I repeat.

I grab the top and bottom of my staff and slam it down with all my might across my right knee. The staff splinters in half. It is now in two pieces. I hold one piece in each hand and lift it in the air.

I hear gasps and a unified "No!" from the crowd.

I hear another bang. Another gunshot. I feel pain again in my chest. I look in the crowd and see a man near the stage holding a handgun. He shot me! I look down and see more blood seeping out of my chest.

I raise the two pieces of Aaron's staff and yell, "Heal me!"

Nothing happens.

The pain persists. The blood continues to run out of my body. I see officers arresting the shooter.

"Help," I whisper as I crumble to the ground.

CHAPTER 26

The sharp pain in my chest spreads through the rest of my being. I gasp. Breathing is suddenly a chore. I feel life quickly leaving my body. I look up at Anna. She leans over and screams for help. She's crying. She puts her hands over my wound and presses down.

"We need paramedics over here! Now!" she yells.

I'm confused. Why didn't the staff heal me? Why did God abandon me? Then I realize the truth. When I broke the staff, I gave up God's powers. Why am I so stupid? God gave me His powers and I blew it. I screwed everything up.

I reach up and put my hand to Anna's wet cheek. "It's okay," I say. I use my thumb to wipe away her tears. "I know where I'm going."

"But I don't want you to go," she says. Her voice cracks. "I need you."

"I love you," is all I can say. Blood fills my lungs. "I'm dying," I cough. "I'll miss you."

"I'll miss you, too," Anna says. "I love you so much." She grabs my hand and squeezes. I try to squeeze back but don't have the strength.

My heart stops. As my final breath leaves my body, scenes from my life flash through my mind. My childhood. Meeting Anna.

Our wedding. Our son. Vacations. Happy times together. I see them all.

I then feel my soul rip away from my physical body. It doesn't hurt, but I am now free from the chains of the physical world. Gravity no longer holds me down.

I float above my physical body. The pain is gone. So is my sadness. I see Anna below me, crying, calling for help. I see paramedics rushing up on the stage. I see the shocked look on everyone's faces. I see the shooter wearing a smug smile as officers walk him to a police cruiser. I see people leaving. Some crying. Some smiling. Some sad. Some happy. What a strange scene!

The world in front of me evaporates, and everything turns soft white. I am standing in a different world now. I am no longer on earth. I realize I have crossed over into heaven.

"Hi, Christian." Michael floats toward me, followed by six other angels. My guides. They are all smiling at me. Their soft, white wings glow bright. Michael still wears his golden armor with his sword sheathed, attached to a belt on his side. "Welcome to heaven." I notice his mouth doesn't move. We are speaking through some sort of strange metaphysical connection, where I can hear him in my head. I realize I can talk to him the same way.

"I died," I mentally tell him.

"I know. And I'm sorry. I couldn't save you this time. God's orders."

"God wanted me dead?"

"No, God didn't want you dead, but you made a choice to break the staff. That decision led to your death. In a sense, you made the choice to die. All you had to do was grab Anna and go back to your hotel room and you'd still be alive right now."

"How was I to know another gunman in the crowd would shoot me? You're right, though. I should've left sooner."

"It's okay. What happened, happened. You can't change it now."

"I guess I really screwed up everything, didn't I?"

Michael puts a hand on my shoulder, and peace overcomes me. I look down and discover my body is translucent. White light emanates from my very being. I lift my hands to my face in fascination. I am no longer a slave to the human body. I have shed it for a lighter, brighter vessel. A heavenly body.

I feel regret for my actions on earth.

"You probably could've made some better decisions during your life on earth," Michael says, "especially those last few days when you possessed God's powers. But that's what living is all about. It's about figuring out what you did wrong and then learning from your mistakes."

"I made a lot of them."

"Don't be so hard on yourself. You also made some incredibly wise choices and improved the lives of many people. Like all the kids in the hospital you healed."

"I should've healed more people."

"And you would've, had you not died. But you died. And here you are."

"This experience with God's powers helped me understand God better."

"How so?" Michael asks.

"I know how God feels when people don't believe in him. Unappreciated. Cast aside. Hated."

"And yet, God still loves all the people He's created. Mainly because when they come here, they learn the truth, that God and heaven are real. Even if they don't give Him their love while human, they do once they arrive here."

"But man, people are so mean sometimes."

"I've suggested to God many times that He start over and create people who actually care about Him, but He says that would defeat the purpose."

"Defeat what purpose?"

"Of self-discovery. It would prevent souls from growing. Every single person has a purpose. A reason for being born. God wants every one of His souls to use the talents He gave them to make the world a better place. However, each person is on their own path of self-realization. Each person needs to find the reason behind their existence and then form goals for their life. It's challenging. It's tough navigating a world filled with evil and temptation. It's tough casting all that aside to fulfill God's purpose for you."

"I don't feel like I fulfilled my purpose in this life. I mean, did I even make a difference? I feel like I made the world a worse place, not better."

Michael smiles at me. "You did more good than you realize. Thanks to you, God has decided to give the world a second chance. Many people who doubted His existence now believe in Him thanks to you."

"Really?" I ask.

"Really. You couldn't see it in the moment, but many were moved by your actions these past few days. They saw how you used God's powers to heal and help others, and now they believe in Him. And, because you were assassinated, you will now be a martyr. A symbol of all that's wrong with the world. How people are quick to take down those who challenge their world view rather than taking the time to better understand them. Your death will be used as an example of what happens when people give in to evil and turn away from God.

"But yes, you made a positive impact on the world. It's like when you throw a rock in a lake. You can't see all the ripples, but they still run through the entire lake. The ripples you made will run through the entire world for many years to come and convince many to turn to God."

"I'm so happy to hear this. It's just... I wish more people would've believed in me. Believed that God gave me His powers to do good. I helped so many people, and yet so many people still hated and rejected me."

"Are you surprised?" Michael asked. "I mean, look at Jesus. He also healed many people, and yet some people still hated him and rejected him. At least they didn't throw rocks at you or send you to the cross to be crucified."

"Thank goodness! Are you saying God knew people would reject me like they rejected Jesus?"

Michael shakes his head. "Since God is all-knowing, I'm sure He knew it was a possibility. But no, since God gives people free will, He hoped the people would choose to accept you as His prophet. While most did, a few refused. But again, that was their choice. Hopefully in death, you will now inspire some doubters to find their way to God."

"I hope so," I mumble in my mind. "So, now what?"

"Now we go to paradise, and you get to reunite with your son and all the other people you knew in life who died before you."

"A reunion!"

"Yes, a reunion," Michael says.

"Is Anna going to be okay?" I ask.

"She'll overcome. And someday, you'll be reunited with her right here in heaven. But she still has work to do."

"She does?"

"Yes, she needs to preserve your memory and remind people how God worked through you to bring them closer to Him."

"Can I meet God?" I ask.

"Sure! Grab onto my cloak and I'll take you there."

I reach over, thinking my transparent hand will go right through his translucent cloak, but it doesn't. I grip it and look up at my guardian angel.

"I'm ready."

We float toward the white light in the distance. Joy courses through my being. I can't wait to see what awaits me in heaven.

Made in the USA
Monee, IL
30 April 2025

16507819R00144